A Dream Come True

Jean Ure

RED FOX

DB JF/A C505275499

For Penny Sibson, one of
my very first fans

A Red Fox Book
Published by Random House Children's Books
20 Vauxhall Bridge Road, London SW1V 2SA

A division of Random House UK Ltd
London Melbourne Sydney Auckland
Johannesburg and agencies throughout the world

Copyright © Jean Ure 1994

1   3   5   7   9   10   8   6   4   2

First published in Great Britain by
Hutchinson Children's Books 1994

Red Fox edition 1995

Printed and bound in Great Britain by
Cox & Wyman Ltd, Reading, Berkshire

RANDOM HOUSE UK Limited Reg. No. 954009

ISBN 0 09 925101 9

1

'I shall never have got in, I know I shan't! Miss Porter was looking *daggers*.'

'I nearly died when Madam walked in!'

'You know that bit she gave us, right at the end – '

'*Fondu – retiré – *'

Jessamy, blithely disregarding the curious gazes of the other passengers on the district line tube, dumped her bag and began dancing her way across the carriage.

Jessamy was like that; a bit of a show-off, according to some people. It came from having a famous family and being used to being the centre of attention. *Jessamy Hart, daughter of prima ballerina Belinda Tarrant and premier danseur Ben Hart – sister of Saul, golden boy of City Ballet.*

Oh, Jessamy had it made! You couldn't go wrong, thought Karen – wistfully, but not enviously – as she watched Jessamy perform a series of lightning-fast turns practically on the spot.

Serve her right if the train came to a sudden halt was what Tammy Chopping thought, though not with any particular rancour. To be fair to Jessamy, she never paraded the fact that her mum and dad were famous. And anyway, the more pushy you were, the more chance you stood of making it. No use hiding your light under a toadstool, or whatever the saying was; no one would ever bother to come seeking you out. This game was about self-advertisement.

'I got absolutely *lost*!' wailed Margaret Moorhouse, more commonly known as Maggot.

'I don't expect you were the only one,' said Karen, comfortingly.

'Well, but I bet you didn't!'

Karen was one of those lucky people who had only to see a step demonstrated once to have it fixed for all time in her very bones. Maggot, who wasn't blessed with that kind of instant memory, always kept an eye on her in class and tried to follow her if she found herself in difficulties. Karen might not be as showy as Jessamy, but she was a far neater dancer; far more delicate and precise. Jessamy, on the other hand, though she could be slapdash, had the art of carrying off her mistakes with such an air that she could quite often fool people into not noticing that she had made any. It wasn't wise to follow Jessamy; people with less glittering personalities could quickly come to grief.

'They expect a *few* mistakes,' said Karen. 'They don't expect us to be perfect.'

'No, and they don't expect us to mess up on a perfectly simple sequence,' moaned Maggot.

'I don't think you should let it worry you. It's just one of those things. It can happen to anyone.'

'It's all right you saying that! You didn't go and mess up on anything!'

'That yellow thing did. Honestly,' shrieked Jessamy, coming to a dramatic halt, one hand on her hip, the other flung up behind her, 'I nearly died when she tripped over her own feet!'

'I nearly died when I got lost,' said Maggot.

Nella Stevens, dark and serious, half Italian with luminous black eyes which Jessamy secretly envied, shook her head, reproachfully.

'There's no sense brooding. You'll only upset yourself.'

'I already have upset myself! And I'll never get in, anyway; I'm the wrong shape.'

The others turned, doubtfully, to consider her. It was true that Maggot wasn't tall and skinny like Tamara, or small and slender like Nella and Karen, in fact if she put on too much weight she would be decidedly short and dumpy, but 'You've got good strong legs for jumping,' said Jessamy, who had good strong legs herself.

'What would you do if you didn't get in?' Tammy floated the question in the air, addressing it seemingly to the carriage at large.

Maggot screamed. 'Don't! I can't bear it!'

It wasn't the sort of question that a person should ask. Trust Tammy! She was almost as brash as Jessamy.

'What my mum says,' said Nella, 'is what's done is done and there's no point in worrying.'

'I'm not worried,' said Jessamy.

'I am,' said Karen.

'*You*?' Maggot looked at her as if she had gone mad. 'You've got nothing to worry about! You'll get in.'

Jessamy frowned slightly; so did Tammy. Karen, as usual, turned rather pink.

'When do you think they'll let us know?'

'In about a week,' said Tammy, 'according to Miss Porter.'

'A week!' howled Maggot. 'I can't bear it!'

The train reached Victoria, which was where Maggot and Nella got off.

'Give us a ring,' shouted Maggot, 'as soon as you hear!'

The train doors slid together; the train moved on. There was a silence.

'Poor old Maggot,' said Tammy, at last.

'Do you think Maggot *will* get in?' said Karen, as she and Jessamy left the train at Chiswick Park.

Jessamy hunched a shoulder. 'Stranger things have been known.'

It would be dreadful, thought Karen, soberly, if they all got in except for Maggot. Or, she thought, except for me! The five of them – Jessamy Hart, Karen Anders, Nella Stevens, Tammy Chopping, Maggot Moorhouse – had been attending the Saturday morning associate classes at the City Ballet School for the past year. They were all of them dedicated; Miss Porter wouldn't have put them in for the audition if she hadn't felt they were serious. Not all the associate pupils wanted to become full-time dance students. Some hadn't yet made up their minds, some actually wanted to finish their ordinary schooling first. Karen found that almost incredible. Imagine preferring to stay on at ordinary school when you could be going to ballet school!

Jessamy, with an exaggerated sigh, said, 'I *suppose* I'll get in.'

Karen looked at her, uncertainly. It sounded horribly like boasting, yet Jessamy wasn't boastful. It was true she didn't suffer from false modesty, but as against that she always admitted when she was bad at things (usually things such as maths and home economics where she didn't think it mattered). All the same, Karen was glad she hadn't said it in front of the others. Karen knew her better than they did; they might have thought she needed taking down a peg or two.

'Well, of *course* you'll get in,' said Karen. It was quite unthinkable that she shouldn't. Not only did she come from a ballet family, but she had been taught by her own mother – and Belinda Tarrant was every bit as gifted a teacher as she had been a dancer. Impossible that Jessamy wouldn't be offered a place!

'I know.' Jessamy heaved another sigh. 'If it was life and death I probably wouldn't. But when you don't specially care – '

'Jessamy!' Karen stared at her, shocked. 'How can you say that?'

'Well, I don't,' said Jessamy. 'Not really; not like you do. I mean – '

She pushed her hair back. Karen's hair, fine and blond and straight, was still pulled into its classical bun the way she wore it for class. Jessamy's, thick, dark brown, and just a little bit curly, was flowing loose about her shoulders. The first thing Jessamy always did after class was set her hair free. She didn't feel the need to parade her identity as a dancer, the way Karen did. (But that was because Jessamy had always been a dancer: Karen had had to fight to be one.)

'I mean I'd rather be at ballet school than stay on at Coombe Hurst, obviously. It's just that – well! Ballet isn't the *only* thing in life. I wouldn't go out and drown myself or anything if they didn't take me. But of course they will.' She said it almost gloomily. 'I've been

11

marked out for it from the word go. It's like it's my destiny and I can't escape it.'

'Would you really want to?' said Karen. '*Really*?'

'I'd like to think that I'd chosen it,' said Jessamy, 'instead of it choosing me. That's why you feel differently, because you *did* choose it.'

'Yes, and it's the only, only thing I want to do and if I don't get in I'll – I'll – ' Karen clenched both fists. 'I don't know what!'

'Oh, you'll get in all right,' said Jessamy. 'You're one of Mum's pupils. Mum's pupils always get in. She doesn't let them try unless she's a hundred per cent sure. Her *reputation*,' said Jessamy. 'She'd never get over it if they had the nerve to turn someone down.'

'Haven't they ever?' said Karen.

'No!' Jessamy giggled. 'That's 'cause they're all scared of her.'

'It's because she's a good teacher,' said Karen. 'But I don't expect any of her other pupils have had to get scholarships.' She regarded Jessamy, hopefully. 'Have they?'

'Mm . . . n-no.' Jessamy rubbed the bridge of her nose as she thought about it. 'Maybe not.'

'They only give two scholarships a year!'

'You might be able to get a grant, though,' said Jessamy.

She knew that Karen's gran, whom she lived with, couldn't afford to pay for her. Right at the start she hadn't even been able to afford lessons just once a week with Belinda Tarrant; Karen had had to be given them free. But then old Mrs Anders, who was rather proud, had decided she couldn't go on accepting charity and so she had let out the whole top floor of her house to students, while she and Karen crammed into the ground floor and even shared a bedroom. Karen's gran had made great sacrifices to let her have her ballet lessons; it would be too awful if Karen were offered a place and couldn't take it up for lack of funds.

'Don't worry,' said Jessamy, 'even if they don't give you an actual scholarship – ' and really you would have to be incredibly and outstandingly promising to get one of those, and she didn't honestly think Karen was *that* outstanding – 'I'm sure Mum would manage to find a way.'

Jessamy had great faith in Belinda Tarrant's powers. The difficulty lay in rousing her interest. To begin with, for instance, she had positively refused to listen when Jessamy had told her how brilliant Karen would be if she could only afford to have proper lessons. It wasn't until Saul had stepped in that she had sat up and taken notice. Once she had actually seen for herself what Karen could do, she had moved heaven and earth to convince Mrs Anders that her granddaughter had the makings of a dancer.

'Mum'll get you a grant,' said Jessamy. 'She'll go and talk to someone.' It was what Belinda Tarrant was always saying: *I shall go and talk to someone.* 'And when she's talked to them they'll agree to pay your fees and everything 'cause they'll know that you're going to be a good investment.'

Karen giggled, a bit nervously. 'I haven't been offered a place yet!'

'Oh, you'll get a place! So will Tammy; they like dancers that are tall and skinny. And Nella, 'cause she looks right. And me, 'cause I just bet you. 'Cause it's fate and it's going to happen whether I like it or not. Mag's the only one I'm not sure about. Stranger things *have* been known – '

Jessamy didn't actually add the word 'but': she didn't have to. They both felt there was a question mark hanging over Maggot; funny little round-faced, short-legged Maggot.

Jessamy shook her head. 'You can't really see her dancing Giselle, can you?'

'No, but you always said that you couldn't dance Giselle,' pointed out Karen.

Jessamy drew herself up, rather haughtily. 'That is because I have the wrong *temperament*; not because I am a *midget*. And I do think I could dance the Sleeping Princess, for instance, if I wanted to. *If* I wanted to. I might not want to. But who could she ever dance?'

'She could do modern,' said Karen.

'Not at City Ballet, she couldn't. I really don't know,' said Jessamy, 'why Miss Porter put her in for it. It's only raising false hopes.'

'Well, anyway,' said Karen. She hesitated. 'See you tomorrow? In class?'

Jessamy pulled a face. 'I suppose so.'

It was the start of the Easter holidays, but the idea of letting them have a day off was something which wouldn't occur to Belinda Tarrant. If Jessamy and Karen were going to be professional dancers, then they should observe a professional dancer's routine. That meant class *every single day* – except, thank goodness, Sunday. Even Belinda Tarrant relaxed on Sunday, though Jessamy sometimes suspected she would like

Sunday opening for ballet schools just as there was Sunday opening for shops. Karen probably wouldn't object to it, either.

Karen was so single-minded, thought Jessamy; her entire life revolved round the ballet. Ask her the name of the Prime Minister and she would have to stop and think about it, but ask her who did the choreography for, say, the *Three-Cornered Hat* and she would come right out with it: Leonid Massine. No problem.

Belinda Tarrant would approve of that. She would say it showed a proper dedication. If you asked Jessamy, it was a bit scary. It was doing what Mrs Richmond, their English teacher, had said you shouldn't ever do, which was put all your eggs in one basket. If Karen didn't get into ballet school her entire world would collapse; whereas Jessamy –

Jessamy stepped out boldly as the light on the pedestrian crossing turned green. Jessamy didn't believe in being obsessed. There were other things in life besides ballet. Acting, for instance; Jessamy often thought that she would like to be an actress. If she didn't get into ballet school she could always go to drama school, Italia Conti, or somewhere that took you when you were still only thirteen. There must be lots of them.

But of course Jessamy *would* get into ballet school. She did a hop, skip and jump along the pavement. Mum would have her guts for garters if she didn't!

2

For once, Belinda Tarrant was in when Jessamy arrived home. She was in the front room; Jessamy could hear her talking to someone in her light, crisp tones.

'Saul, my dear – ' oh, so Saul was here as well! Jessamy brightened. She always liked it when Saul paid them a visit. 'Saul, my dear, I wasn't born yesterday, you know. I am really quite unshockable. In any case, it's your life. I wouldn't dream of – '

She broke off as Jessamy appeared.

'Here she comes again,' said Saul, 'crashing about where she's not wanted.'

'Why aren't I wanted?' Jessamy was indignant. 'Are you talking secrets?'

'Having what we fondly believed was a private conversation.'

'Talking secrets,' said Jessamy.

'Certainly no concern of yours,' agreed Saul.

Jessamy thought about it. 'Are you saying that you'd like me to go away?'

'Would I say a thing like that?' said Saul.

'I will if you really insist,' said Jessamy, 'but I think it would be a bit mean considering I've only just got here *and* I happen to live here, which is more than you do – *and* I've just taken my assessment class.'

'In that case –' Saul, spreadeagled on the sofa, waved a hand. 'Feel free!'

Jessamy needed no second invitation: she bounced down beside him. Karen would be sick as a parrot if she knew that Saul was here and she had missed him. Saul was one of her heroes – Rudolf Nureyev, Mikhail Baryshnikov, and Saul. Saul was lots of people's hero. Rather sickening, really, but Jessamy supposed (trying to see him through eyes other than those of a sister) that he was quite good-looking, as well as being a brilliant dancer. She was used to people fawning on him.

'So how did you get on?' Belinda Tarrant wanted to know.

'All right,' said Jessamy.

'How about Karen?'

'She got on all right, except she's fussed about what's going to happen if she doesn't get a scholarship.'

'Oh, I've already thought of that! As soon as we receive official notification I'll have a word with someone.'

'Do we sound,' ventured Saul, cocking an eyebrow, 'rather sure of ourselves?'

Belinda Tarrant spoke briskly. 'I don't anticipate either of these two girls being turned down!'

'What were you and Saul talking secrets about?' said Jessamy, later.

'Nothing to do with you!' said her mum.

'People shouldn't talk secrets, it's rude.'

'Only when they do it in front of people. We,' pointed

17

out Belinda Tarrant, 'were doing it all on our own until you came bursting in.'

Jessamy, disgruntled, said, 'I thought you'd be waiting to hear how the assessment class had gone.' Any normal mother would. She sometimes thought that hers just took things for granted.

'Darling, of course I want to hear! But I didn't really imagine it would be any different from your normal class.'

'Well, it was,' said Jessamy. 'Madam took us for it. It was so funny! Everyone just *froze* when she walked in. Some people,' said Jessamy, 'are really frightened of her.'

Madam – whose real name was Natalya de Savary, except that since last New Year's honours list she had been made Dame Natalya, 'for services to the dance' – was one of the founders of City Ballet. Belinda Tarrant had been one of her first pupils, and one of the first 'home-grown' ballerinas to emerge from the ranks of the corps de ballet. Jessamy had known Madam since she was a tiny child – well, not exactly known, perhaps; Madam was too grand for that, and too remote. But at least she didn't send shivers down Jessamy's spine as she did with most of the others.

'Honestly,' said Jessamy, 'they *shook*.'

'And so they should!' retorted Belinda Tarrant. 'I shook whenever she took class. I should still shake today. A little more respect from you, my girl, might not go amiss!' Then she swept out of the room.

Well, thought Jessamy, but it was silly to be scared of people – and she didn't believe her mum *would*

18

shake. Mum wasn't that sort of person, any more than Jessamy was.

'Maggot rang me up last night,' said Karen, as she and Jessamy changed for class the next day. 'She's dead worried she's not going to get in.'

'It could be a blessing in disguise,' said Jessamy, wisely. 'Sometimes it's better if people discover the truth early on.'

'But it'll break her heart!' said Karen.

'Can't be helped; it's something you just have to face up to. It doesn't matter how good you are. If you're not the right shape – '

'She might change.' Karen said it doubtfully. 'People *do* change.'

'Pigs might fly,' said Jessamy.

There was nothing sentimental about Jessamy. She believed in facing the facts squarely, tackling problems head on – her own, as well as other people's. If Jessamy were to be turned down, thought Karen, she wouldn't sit and mope, she would instantly decide on some other course of action. But then it just wasn't possible that Jessamy should be turned down. She, out of all of them, was certain to be offered a place – and not just because she was Belinda Tarrant's daughter, but because she was a good dancer with lashings of personality. Karen sometimes thought rather sadly that she herself didn't have any personality at all; she was just small, insignificant Karen who didn't want to do anything except dance.

If I don't get in, thought Karen, determinedly, I shan't give up. She would still go on taking lessons from Belinda Tarrant. But it would be the most terrible struggle for Gran to go on finding enough money to pay for classes. Two, or even three a week, wouldn't be enough. She would need one every day. Jessamy was so lucky! She had been learning ballet since she was four years old. No wonder she could be so relaxed about it.

'Yessamy!' Marisol, the Spanish au pair who had replaced German Elke, called to Jessamy up the stairs. 'There is Karen on the telephone for you. You take it in your room?'

'OK!' Jessamy lunged across the bed and clawed up the receiver. 'Hi!'

'Jessamy? It's me,' said Karen. She sounded all breathless and squeaky.

'I know it's you! Marisol said it was.'

'Jessamy, I've got it!'

'Got what?' said Jessamy. 'Chicken pox?'

'No! The scholarship!'

'Oh, that is *brilliant*,' said Jessamy. 'That is truly *brilliant*! Of course,' she added, 'I knew that you would.'

'I didn't,' said Karen.

'No, that's because you're too modest. What does your gran think? Is she pleased?'

'She's thrilled!' said Karen. 'She says I've got your mum to thank for it – and you, of course. And – ' Jessamy could almost see her blushing down the telephone – 'and Saul. She says I've got to thank you all properly. She – '

'Yes, yes, yes, never mind all that!' Jessamy was impatient for the details. 'When did you hear?'

'Just now – just this minute. I was almost too scared to open the letter!'

'Daft,' said Jessamy. When hers came, she would rip it open straight away. *When* it came.

'How about you?' said Karen. A note of sudden anxiety entered her voice. 'Haven't you heard yet?'

'Not yet. I expect they do the scholarship people first. I expect I'll get a letter tomorrow.'

'Let me know the minute you do.'

'You bet!' said Jessamy.

Belinda Tarrant purred like a satisfied cat when Jessamy told her the news. She had reason to be satisfied; she, after all, had been prepared to teach Karen for nothing simply because she had had faith in her.

'But what about you?' She looked at Jessamy, sharply. 'Why haven't you heard yet?'

'I wasn't trying for a scholarship,' said Jessamy.

'Well – no; that's true. But I should have thought they'd let everyone know at the same time.'

'I expect they will tomorrow,' said Jessamy.

The next day was Friday and the day after that was Saturday, and Jessamy still hadn't heard. Karen telephoned again to say that 'Maggot's got in! She just rang me.'

'*Maggot*?' said Jessamy.

'Yes, she can't believe it!'

Jessamy couldn't believe it, either. How come Maggot had heard and not her?

'Haven't they . . .' Karen's voice faltered into silence.

'It's probably got lost in the post,' said Jessamy. She wasn't having Karen feel sorry for her. 'You know – '

she attempted a bravado that for once she was far from feeling – 'you know what the post office is like.'

'You know,' she said to her mum, when Belinda Tarrant floated downstairs at her customary hour of ten o'clock to sort out the mail, 'you know what the post office is like.'

'Perfectly reliable, as a general rule.'

'That's not what Dad says. Dad says – '

'Your Dad says all kinds of silly things.' Frown lines were already wrinkling Belinda Tarrant's forehead. 'This really is too bad! They said a week – it's been almost ten days. I've a good mind to ring them up.'

'Oh, Mum, no!' If there was one thing Jessamy couldn't bear, it was for her mum to make a fuss; it would look too much like demanding special treatment. 'Wait till Monday,' begged Jessamy. 'It's bound to be here by then.'

Whatever Mum might say, letters *did* get held up. It was strange, all the same; Jessamy couldn't help just a teeny tinge of doubt seeping in. Suppose they hadn't sent the letter because it was bad news and they were leaving it till last?

Imagine having to go back to Coombe Hurst, with everyone knowing that she was a failure! She had as good as told them that she was leaving to become a ballet student, it was what they all expected of her. How could she go on having lessons with Mum, knowing that all the other kids – Wendy Adams, Dawn Collier, Selma Chadwick with her fat thighs – were secretly rejoicing? Belinda Tarrant's daughter, failing her audition for the City Ballet School! Oh, it would be impossible! She couldn't face it! Not only that –

Not only that, in spite of her brave words, *ballet isn't the ONLY thing in life*, Jessamy knew without any doubt whatsoever that it was an extremely important thing. It might be that at the end of the day she would decide to do something different, like becoming an actress, but it had to be *her* decision, not anyone else's.

Karen came round on Sunday to watch some ballet videos. Jessamy did her best but it was not easy being her normal cheerful self. Who would ever have thought that Karen, shy, retiring Karen who wouldn't say boo to an ant, would succeed where Jessamy might have failed?

Jessamy couldn't help remembering that if it hadn't been for her, Karen would never even have had so much as a single ballet lesson, let alone been offered a scholarship. It was Jessamy who had first spotted Karen's potential, Jessamy who had patiently worked to unravel the mystery of where Karen went for classes, only to discover that she didn't go anywhere but was trying to teach herself out of books from the library. It was Jessamy, too, who had sacrificed her part in the end-of-term show at Coombe Hurst, pretending to twist an ankle so that Karen could step in at the last moment and show what she could do – which was when Saul had seen her, and grown enthusiastic.

If it weren't for Jessamy, Karen wouldn't be anywhere!

It would be very hard to sit back and smile if, of the two of them, it was Karen who made it and Jessamy who fell by the wayside.

'I'm sure the letter will come tomorrow,' whispered Karen, as she left to go home.

23

If there was one thing Jessamy couldn't stand, it was people pitying her.

First thing Monday morning, the letter arrived. It was waiting there, on the door mat, when Jessamy came downstairs. It was addressed to her mum, of course, but that wouldn't as a rule have stopped Jessamy from opening it; not when she knew what it was, and that she was the one it was all about. Mum had already agreed that it was only fair Jessamy should be the one to read it first.

This morning, uncharacteristically, she hesitated. Her spine prickled as she picked the letter up. She turned it over, reading the words on the back: City Ballet School, 14–18 Edridge Street, London SE1. Slowly, she slid a finger under the flap. (It was not Jessamy's usual way of opening letters. Her usual way was simply to rip.) Even more slowly she drew out the sheet of paper that was inside. Slower still, she unfolded it.

'*Dear Mrs Hart,*' she read. (It was difficult, sometimes, to remember that Mum was Mrs Hart.)

'*With reference to your daughter Jessamy's recent audition for entry to our Junior Department –* '

The pit of Jessamy's stomach lurched, sickeningly.

– '*I am happy to inform you that she has been selected for a place for the winter term beginning on 15th September. If you wish to accept this offer –* '

'Mum!' yelled Jessamy, racing two at a time up the stairs to her mum's bedroom. 'It's come! I've been accepted!'

'Well, I should hope you have,' said Belinda Tarrant. She hoisted herself up the bed, her red-gold hair fanning out across the pillows. 'Let me have a look.' She held out a hand for the letter. 'Goodness only knows,' she grumbled, 'why it took so long for them to tell us.'

'I knew you had to get in,' said Karen, when Jessamy rang to tell her. There was a note of relief in her voice all the same. How could she have gone to ballet school without Jessamy? Why, if it hadn't been for Jessamy she would still be struggling along on her own! 'But you know who didn't?' said Karen.

'Who?'

'Tammy.'

'*Tammy* didn't?'

'No, it's terrible, she's ever so upset. She was all crying when she rang me.'

Why had she rung Karen? wondered Jessamy. Karen and Tammy weren't special friends. Why ring Karen rather than Jessamy?

'What's she going to do?' said Jessamy.

'She says she's going to stay on at school and try again when she's sixteen.'

'How *awful*.' Jessamy could afford to be sympathetic now that she herself was safe. 'But fancy taking Maggot and not Tammy! It makes you wonder if they know what they're doing.'

'I suppose they have their reasons,' said Karen.

'Maybe Madam took a dislike to her . . . she's very funny that way. I'll give Tam a ring and try to cheer her up.'

'You will be nice to her, won't you?' said Karen.

'Well, of *course* I will,' said Jessamy.

What did Karen think? She was going to crow, or something? She would simply point out that ballet

25

wasn't the only thing in the world. With legs like that, Tammy could probably become a top model.

'Not nearly as much hard work,' Jessamy would say, 'and *loads* more money.'

That would cheer her up.

3

'Wouldn't it be utter heaven,' sighed Karen, 'if we could have dancing classes all day long and not have to bother with boring things like maths and geography?'

'Well, it would,' agreed Jessamy, 'except that people are always going on and on about how dancers need to be *educated*.'

'Dunno what for,' said Maggot. She giggled. She had been giggling ever since she and Nella had met up with Karen and Jessamy on the northern line platform at the Embankment, ready to catch the train to Waterloo and walk to school all together in a bunch. There was safety in numbers, on this very first day of the winter term.

'It's in case you get chucked out and have to start doing something else,' said Jessamy.

Maggot screamed. 'Don't! I can't bear it!'

'Well, I can't think of any other reason . . . I don't see how knowing *algebra* – ' Jessamy said it with loathing: algebra was her current pet hate – 'is going to help anyone dance Juliet or do a better arabesque.'

'I think we should just concentrate on things like art and music,' said Karen, blissfully.

'Yes, and then we could have more time for dancing. Do you realize,' said Maggot, in shocked tones, 'we only have *two hours* a day?'

It was Karen's turn to giggle. Her gran, looking at the timetable for second years, had said, 'Two hours a day? Just dancing?'

'Until we get into seniors.' Jessamy nodded. 'Then we have oceans of it.'

'*If* we get into seniors,' said Nella.

Maggot gave another scream. 'Don't! Don't say things like that!'

'They don't take everybody,' said Nella.

'Look, just try being a bit positive for once,' scolded Jessamy. 'You and Karen are like a couple of wet sponges.'

'I never said a thing!' said Karen.

'No, but you know what you're like . . . always worrying about what's going to happen next instead of enjoying what's happening now.'

'Well, I'm not today,' said Karen. Today she was in her seventh heaven.

The train drew in to Waterloo and they jostled out on to the platform with all the other rush-hour travellers going off to their boring work in offices and shops. Not for me! thought Jessamy, swinging her bag. (At least her bag contained tights and ballet shoes and leotards as well as normal school stuff such as pens and pencils. That was one comfort, even if they were only going to have two hours of dancing a day.)

'I am never *ever* going to do an ordinary sort of job,' said Jessamy.

'Well, I should hope not!' said Karen. 'You're going to be a dancer.'

Or an actress, thought Jessamy.

'Do you know what I'm dreading?' said Nella, as

they crammed out through the automatic barriers. 'That's being new again ... I hate being new!'

'Me, too!' said Karen.

Jessamy groaned. 'There they go! Being new doesn't bother me in the *slightest*,' said Jessamy. 'Just imagine if we were Tammy, having to go back to ordinary school.'

'Oh, don't!' shrieked Maggot. 'It's like a nightmare!'

It was as well that Jessamy was with them, to lead the way confidently down the dark, dank underpass, out into Waterloo Road – terrifyingly wide and full of traffic, but to the east you could see the National Theatre – turn right at Lower Marsh with its rows of small fascinating shops and market stalls, then left into Baylis Road (named after Lilian Baylis, the founder of the Old Vic) and left again, at last, into Edridge Street.

Edridge Street was a cul de sac, with a high brick wall at the end. On the wall someone artistic had painted a colourful mural, depicting scenes from various ballets – Swan Lake, Firebird, Les Sylphides. Right next door was the school itself, three old houses knocked into one, with a sign outside which read:

CITY BALLET SCHOOL
Principal: Natalya de Savary
(Upper Department: no. 14 Lower Department:
nos 16–18)

By the end of term it was all going to be as familiar to Karen as Chiswick, where she lived with her gran; but on this first morning it seemed very strange and alien. Karen had never been there before, for their Saturday morning classes and the audition had taken place at a studio in a quite different part of London. Jessamy, on the other hand, had been paying visits to the school for years, either with Saul or with her mum and dad. Would she be as sure of herself as Jessamy, wondered Karen, if she came from a famous family? Probably not; Jessamy was a very special person in her own right.

The first day at ballet school was a curious mixture of the ordinary and the extraordinary.

The extraordinary, right at the beginning, was a rigorous medical examination involving not just height and weight but a thorough check to ensure that bodies were in good working order and strong enough to withstand all the pressures of the coming weeks. (What disaster, thought Karen, if you were found not to be fit!) It was having ballet on the timetable instead of PE, and ballet studios where in any other school you might have expected a gym or an indoor netball court. It was also a visit from the shoemakers so that pupils could buy sufficient pairs of shoes to last the term – six in Jessamy's case, because her parents were paying and could afford it, only four in Karen's, because that was all her scholarship allowed for. (She would just have to dance lightly, thought Karen, and darn the toes of her point shoes with extra care. She didn't want to have to go to Gran and beg for more money if she could possibly help it.)

The ordinary was the familiar – desks in classrooms, French, geography, *algebra*: attendance registers, homework. Any secret hopes they may have had of being let off lightly from normal schoolwork were dashed right at the beginning by Mrs Enwright, Head of Academic Studies, who gathered all the newcomers together – six second years plus the whole of the first year's intake – and sternly informed them that 'Just because you are ballet students does not mean you can afford to neglect your general education.'

Jessamy turned and pulled a face at Karen.

'You will all work towards your GCSEs, and no slacking will be tolerated. I feel it's wise to make this quite clear at the outset, as we have in the past had students who felt it was perfectly possible to become a successful dancer with a head totally devoid of all knowledge. This,' said Mrs Enwright, looking rather hard at Jessamy, 'is a fallacy. We shall expect you to devote as much attention to your academic studies as to your vocational ones. Please bear it in mind.'

'She can't be serious,' whispered Jessamy, as they filed out.

Karen thought that most probably she wasn't; she was just warning them that they wouldn't be allowed to get away with not doing their homework or being late for class. She couldn't honestly believe that anyone in their right senses would care as much about theorems and glacier formation as they did about the quality of their *ports de bras* or the height of their extension.

All that was the ordinary, and really not so very different from normal school except that (a) there were boys (there hadn't been any boys at Coombe Hurst), and (b) all the girls were slim and shapely and had long hair. It was a little odd, at first, not to look round the class and see the plump and the lumpy and the gangling and ungainly. It rather put you in your place, thought Karen; made you realize you were just one amongst many.

She felt even more that she was just one amongst many when they had their first ballet class with Miss

31

Eldon, assistant Head of Dance. Even at the Saturday morning associate classes, which were selected strictly according to ability, there had always been some who were quite obviously not going to make the grade. If it hadn't exactly given you a superiority complex, it had at least made you feel that perhaps you were a little bit special or different. Here at the City Ballet School it seemed to Karen, at any rate on a first showing, that *everyone* was capable of making it and that several people were of a far higher standard than she could ever dream of reaching.

She confided her fears to Maggot, afterwards, knowing that Maggot would be humble enough to agree with her.

'Oh, I know!' shrieked Maggot, ever obliging. 'Isn't it ghastly?' Maggot had long since stopped giggling. 'It made me feel like some horrible stodgy pudding, just *plopping* everywhere. Especially that girl with the red hair – '

'Ginny Alexander.'

'She's brilliant,' moaned Maggot. 'I couldn't take my eyes off her! Did you notice the way Miss Eldon kept calling her to the front?'

'Mm,' Karen nodded, ruefully. Favouritism, some might say; but there was no denying the girl with red hair had the most prodigious technique. 'Of course, technique isn't everything,' said Karen.

'But it would be nice to have it,' said Maggot.

They sighed, together.

'Not that you have anything to worry about,' said Maggot. 'There's nothing wrong with your technique.'

Karen pulled a face.

32

'Well there isn't! You mightn't be quite as showy, but then you're what I call more of a lyrical dancer.'

'Yes, and you're character,' said Karen, loyally.

'But it's so awfully limiting,' wailed Maggot, 'if one can't even do the steps!'

Karen didn't say anything to Jessamy about Ginny Alexander and her prodigious technique. Jessamy was never humble and in fact had already told Karen off for being too modest and letting herself be pushed around by that very same Ginny. It had been in the morning, after their introductory lecture by Mrs Enwright. The six new second years – Karen, Jessamy, Nella, Maggot and a couple of boys called Jason Berry and Nicky Scott – had been sent off to their classroom, which was Room 1 in Cora Lamb. (The three old houses were all known by different names – Cora Lamb, Madam's and Middle. Cora Lamb was named after a famous dancer who had left money in her will. They were connected by a maze of stairs and passageways which Karen just knew she was never going to find her way around.)

The six of them had reached Room 1 at the same time as the rest of the class. Jessamy, with her usual aplomb, had gone surging in at the head of the throng: Karen, rather more meekly, had let herself be elbowed to one side.

'Karen! Quick!' Jessamy had waved impatiently at her from the back of the room. 'I've saved a seat for you!'

Too late. Before Karen could get there, red-haired Ginny had bagged it for one of her friends. Jessamy had been furious. In order to sit together, she and

Karen had had to move down to the front, which was not at all what Jessamy had planned.

'You really must learn to stand up for yourself,' she grumbled. 'You'll never get anywhere if you just let people walk all over you.'

'It's difficult when you're new.' Karen had said it apologetically. You couldn't just march into a place and start throwing your weight around.

The argument, predictably, had cut no ice with Jessamy.

'It doesn't make any *difference*. We've got just as much right to be here as she has.'

Karen had a feeling that Ginny and Jessamy were fated to cross swords. They were too much alike; both forceful personalities, used to getting their own way.

At lunch time in the canteen, while Karen was waiting for Jessamy to join her in the queue, she found herself approached by Ginny and her friend Lorraine Hooper.

'D'you mind me asking you something?' said Ginny. 'D'you mind me asking why it is you've only just come here?'

'Is it because you tried last year and failed?' said Lorraine.

Karen shook her head. 'My gran had to have time to get used to the idea.'

'Your gran?'

'What's it to do with your gran?'

'I live with her.'

'So why did she have to get used to the idea?'

'Well, because I only started proper lessons when I was eleven.'

Karen knew as soon as she had said it that she shouldn't have done. Lorraine's eyes widened, Ginny's lip curled.

'Eleven? That's ridiculous! Eleven's far too late.'

'I know it is a *bit* late,' said Karen.

'A bit?' Ginny hooted. 'It's practically geriatric!'

'What about the others?' said Lorraine. 'I suppose they didn't start till they were geriatric, either.'

'Judging by their *dancing*,' said Ginny. 'That little dumpy one – '

'Maggot?' Karen felt a flash of indignation. How dare this horrible person refer to Maggot as dumpy!

'Whatever her name is. What does she think she's doing here?'

As coldly as she could (which wasn't very cold: Karen wasn't very good at being cold), Karen said, 'She took an audition, the same as the rest of us. And the reason she didn't come last year was because she was living in Germany.'

'That shouldn't stop you. We've got people from all over. Australia – '

'New Zealand.'

'*China*.'

'What about the pushy one?'

'The one that thinks she's the dog's dinner.'

They sniggered. Jessamy had obviously already made enemies.

'Why not ask her yourself?' said Karen.

'Ask me what?' demanded Jessamy, bounding across the canteen.

'They want to know why you didn't come here earlier.'

Jessamy raised both her eyebrows. 'What's it to do with them?'

'My! Aren't we hoity toity?' said Ginny.

She and Lorraine exchanged glances.

'Well, if she won't tell us,' said Lorraine, 'we just have to assume that she didn't get in first time round.'

'Or perhaps she hadn't started lessons?' suggested Ginny. 'Perhaps she was another geriatric.'

Jessamy turned away, not deigning to reply.

'Jessamy's been learning since she was four years old!' said Karen. 'She could have come here any time she liked.'

'So why didn't she?'

''Cause her sister went to the Royal Ballet School when she was eleven and got into City Ballet and then gave it up to have babies and her mum wanted to make sure that Jessamy knew what she was doing before she did it.'

'Oh, really?' Ginny suppressed a yawn. 'And who was her sister? Anyone we've heard of?'

'Jacquetta Hart.'

'Don't know her.'

'I bet you know their mum and dad!' Karen never minded boasting on Jessamy's behalf. 'Their dad is Ben Hart and their mum is Belinda Tarrant. And their *brother* – ' Karen felt her cheeks fire up: she could never mention Saul's name without turning stupidly scarlet – 'their brother is *Saul* Hart.' And nobody but nobody that was into ballet could say they hadn't heard of Saul Hart.

There was a pause; then Ginny, recovering herself,

said, '*That* tells a tale. Now we know how she got in!'

'Don't we just?' said Lorraine.

The two of them picked up their trays and swept away.

'I really can't imagine,' said Jessamy, 'why you bothered talking to them.'

'I wanted them to know who you were.'

'I'm not *anyone*,' said Jessamy. 'Yet.'

She clattered a knife and fork on to her tray. One day she would be someone, and it wouldn't be Belinda Tarrant's daughter or Saul Hart's sister, it would be *Jessamy Hart*. She didn't believe in basking in reflected glory – especially when it gave ammunition to the likes of Ginny Alexander. She was bound to go round telling everyone that Jessamy Hart had swanked about her family. Karen meant well, but there were times when she could be the most awful ninny. Jessamy could have told her that a girl of Ginny's type would not be easily impressed. Jessamy herself wouldn't; it was a matter of principle.

On the tube going home at the end of the day she lectured Karen about it.

'Why should she care who my mum and dad are? Why should she care that Saul's my brother?'

'Well, she does!' For once, Karen refused to be repentant. 'She's only pretending not to.'

'How do you know?'

''Cause I saw the inside of her locker, and guess what?'

'What?'

Karen laughed, exultantly. 'She's got a photo of Saul stuck inside it!'

4

'Hallo, Jessamy!'

'Morning, Jess!'

The greetings came from Gemma Dugard and Alessandro Corelli, both leading soloists with City Ballet, as they passed through the main hall of the school on their way to morning rehearsal. Jessamy grinned, and raised her point shoes in salute; not in the least abashed, or, seemingly, flattered. Ginny turned to Lorraine and pulled a face. One or two of the others raised their eyebrows.

It was not unusual for dancers from the Company to use one of the school's studios to rehearse in; what *was* unusual was that any of them should deign to acknowledge a mere student – and a lowly second year, at that! Members of the corps, perhaps, might wave to ex-classmates. But *soloists* –

It wasn't going to do very much for Jessamy's popularity, thought Karen, ruefully. Already people were complaining that Jessamy had gone round boasting about her family, which was totally untrue and unfair, for Jessamy never boasted. It was Karen who had done the boasting, and Jessamy who was paying the price.

It didn't help that Jessamy had the sort of flamboyant personality that drew attention to itself, which was part of the reason that people like Gemma Dugard and

Alessandro Corelli took notice of her; but since they *had* taken notice, it was difficult to see how she was supposed to respond. What did Ginny expect her to do? Go down on her knees and grovel? Ginny didn't seem to realize that Jessamy had known some of the Company dancers since they were students and she was a child. They were as familiar to her as – as aunts and uncles probably were to Ginny. Or perhaps she did realize, and resented it. But that wasn't Jessamy's fault.

Jessamy wasn't a groveller and she wasn't a boaster: she was just Jessamy.

'Hi, you two!'

Saul had come flying through the main entrance door. He waved briefly at Jessamy and Karen – at Karen! He had remembered her! – as he dashed past.

'Hey, Saul – '

'Can't stop!' Saul shot two at a time up the stairs. 'I'm late!'

'But I want to ask you something!'

Jessamy, irrepressible as ever, shot after him. Of course he was her brother; but all the same, thought Karen, struggling to subdue the usual hot tomato of her cheeks – he had recognized her! He had actually *recognized* her! – you would have thought, in front of other people, she would treat him with a bit more respect. After all, he was a leading dancer.

Ginny tossed her head. 'Unspeakable manners, some people have.'

'He's her brother,' said Karen.

'I don't see that's any reason to go shrieking after him just because people are watching her.'

The second years, undoubtedly impressed yet not

40

altogether quite sure that they approved – such behaviour had to come under the category of showing off – moved in a bunch along the corridor towards Cora Lamb and maths with Mr Underdown. Angelique Samuels sidled up to Karen.

'Do you know him?' she whispered.

'Who? Saul?' Karen did her best to throw the name off casually, but still her cheeks sizzled and hissed. (Really, they grew so terribly hot that you could almost fry an egg on them.) 'I've met him round at Jessamy's,' she mumbled.

'What's he like?'

'He's nice.'

'Is he very grand?'

'Not a bit!' It would be difficult to think of anyone less grand than Saul. Belinda Tarrant was grand, and Ben Hart, too, in his own way – Jessamy's dad could be very cutting, very sarcastic, when the mood was on him – but Saul was always good-natured and friendly.

'Don't tell Jessamy –' Angie moved her lips closer to Karen's ear – 'but when I was younger I used to have a thing about her brother.'

What she meant was that she still had a thing. Karen knew the symptoms well enough.

'It's all right,' she said, kindly. 'Jessamy's used to it.'

She had once said carelessly to Karen, 'Oh, everybody's got a thing about Saul. He keeps getting all these love letters from people. Men *and* women.' Karen had been a bit shocked at the time, at the thought of men writing love letters to Saul, but she wasn't any more. It almost seemed quite natural, really. How could anyone *not* write love letters to someone who was so beautiful and danced so divinely?

'I got his autograph once.' Angie sighed, blissfully, at the memory. 'The Company came to Sidney and I queued up outside the stage door and he asked me my name and wrote *To Angelique, with Best Wishes*, and smiled at me.'

'Ginny had a photo of him in her locker at the start of term,' said Karen, 'but she took it down when she found out that Jessamy was his sister.'

'She's just jealous,' said Angie. 'Specially as Jessamy looks like him.'

'Yes, I *know*. She's so *lucky*.'

Both Saul and Jessamy had the most wondrously thick dark curls and what Karen's gran called 'high complexions', which simply meant that instead of being all pale and pasty they had some natural colour in their cheeks. Karen would have loved to have a high complexion. She sometimes thought of herself as looking a bit like skimmed milk (except when she was frying eggs, and that was just embarrassing). She would also have loved to have dark hair and eyes, because everyone knew that brunettes came across the footlights better than blonds. How many truly great dancers had been blond? She bet hardly any. Jessamy said it would be great for the Queen of the Wilis, but she didn't want to dance the Queen of the Wilis, she wanted to dance Giselle!

Jessamy came zooming after them, down the corridor.

'I asked him!'

'Asked him what?'

Jessamy waited till Angie was out of earshot.

'Asked him if there's any chance we might get to be Ice Maidens in the Christmas show.'

'Jessamy, you *didn't*?' Karen stared at her, appalled.

'I did!'

'What did he say?'

Jessamy giggled. 'Told me not to be cheeky!'

'Well, I'm not surprised! It's Madam who decides who's going to be in the Christmas show. And it won't be any of us, anyway. We've only just started.'

'So what?' Jessamy twirled, airily, in the corridor, nearly catching Lorraine a blow with her free hand. 'Nothing ventured, nothing gained.'

'But it's like saying just because he's your *brother* –'

'Pooh, fiddlesticks!' said Jessamy. 'I don't see that it hurts . . . if Madam *did* happen to say to him, "I can't decide who to use from the school, have you got any ideas?" I don't see why he shouldn't make some suggestions. In any case, it wasn't as if I was just asking for me. I was asking for all of us – us four, that is. Not other people.'

'Oh, but Jessamy, you mustn't!' begged Karen 'If –' she lowered her voice – 'if Ginny and Lorraine got to hear of it, they'd go round telling everyone you'd begged for favours.'

'Well, I haven't! I just said a word in the right place. A word in the right place,' said Jessamy, 'works wonders.' That was what Belinda Tarrant always said. 'But anyway, you needn't get in a flap 'cause Madam always makes her own mind up. She never listens to other people.'

'So why did you bother?'

'Oh, well! You never know,' said Jessamy. 'You have to try everything in this business.'

There was great excitement three weeks into term when Madam herself came to take a class. She turned up unexpectedly, because that was Madam's way. She didn't believe in giving advance warning. She couldn't seriously expect to catch anyone out in some heinous crime, such as wearing the wrong colour tights or leotard, for Miss Eldon was quite a martinet about things like that, so maybe what she enjoyed was the slight shiver of apprehension that ran through the class as she appeared. (Surely not even Jessamy could be *totally* immune?)

Madam was a tiny, sharp-featured woman stalking on the highest heels anyone had ever seen. (Woe betide any of her pupils who tried wearing heels like that!) She was dressed, just as she always was, in a little black suit trimmed with silver thread, with a black-and-silver scarf wound about her neck. She wasn't a widow, for she had never married, but no one had ever seen Madam in anything but black.

Miss Eldon, who had barely entered the room before Madam came stalking in, hovered in the background, frowning and grimacing and making furious gestures at anyone who might give offence – at Jessamy, a lock of whose hair had escaped from its mooring; at Angelique Samuels, who hadn't secured her shoe ribbons properly so that the ends were sticking out instead of being neatly tucked in. ('Whiskers', they were called, and were strictly not allowed.)

Madam gave her orders in a light, high, slightly nasal

voice which sounded like royalty but wasn't always easy to understand until you got used to it. When she instructed them to do 'Pliés in first', for example, it came out as 'Pleeyays in farst', which caused nervous people such as Maggot to roll their eyes in terror and watch frantically to see what the person in front was going to do. (The person in front of Maggot happened to be Jessamy, who could fortunately translate what Madam said into ordinary everyday speech and wouldn't have been panicked even if she couldn't.)

'But honestly,' wailed Maggot, afterwards, 'I thought she said do pliés *fast!*'

'I know, and it took me *ages* to work out that crahzay meant croisée,' said Nella. 'I'd have died if I'd been Karen!'

Karen, for some reason, seemed to have taken Madam's fancy. She had been called out to the front and once even asked to demonstrate.

'Goodness knows why,' said Karen, as she and Jessamy waited together on Waterloo platform for a tube.

If anyone else had said 'Goodness knows why' Jessamy would have known at once that they were fishing for compliments. But Karen wasn't like that. When Karen said goodness knows why, she genuinely meant it. It was rather annoying, when Jessamy was secretly harbouring feelings of jealous resentment (why Karen? Karen as opposed to anyone else?). It was difficult to feel resentment against someone who was so earnestly self-effacing.

'I suppose she had her reasons,' said Jessamy.

'Maybe because I'm one of the shortest. Maybe she couldn't see me properly.'

That was one of the stupidest reasons Jessamy had ever heard.

'Maybe because she thought you were *good*,' said Jessamy. 'Maybe she thought you were the best one there.'

Karen's cheeks instantly did their hot tomato act.

'Most probably thought I was the *worst*.'

'Oh, stop being so modest!' cried Jessamy.

Modesty really didn't get you anywhere. You needed to be able to recognize your strengths as well as your weaknesses.

The following week, Miss Eldon announced that a 'radio person' was coming to interview them for a programme about ballet students.

'She'll probably want to ask you questions about how long you've been learning ballet, how you came to do ballet in the first place, how long you've been at the school, what it's like being a ballet student ... all that sort of thing. So just be natural and talk to her as you would to anyone else.'

Jessamy found it quite easy to be natural. She enjoyed talking to the radio person; she could have gone on talking all afternoon, telling her about her mum and dad, and Saul and Jacquetta – 'A real ballet family!' – and how she herself had been having ballet lessons since the age of four. Some of the others were too bashful, or too tongue-tied in front of a microphone.

'You ought to interview Karen,' said Jessamy. 'She's got a really interesting story.' But Karen blushed and shook her head and said she couldn't possibly. It was so silly! How could anyone be shy, talking about themselves? In Jessamy's experience, talking about yourself was the easiest thing in the world.

On the other hand, when a photographer visited the school, wanting photographs of ballet students to illustrate a book, it was Karen whom he picked on without any prompting at all. To begin with, while they were waiting for class to begin and were all busy doing their individual warm-up exercises, working on those parts of their bodies which needed the most attention, he concentrated mainly on Ginny and Jessamy, but once the class was under way it was very noticeably Karen he kept focusing his camera on. Certain people, afterwards, couldn't refrain from commenting.

'I thought he was supposed to be taking pictures of everybody?'

'Is she getting *paid* for it?'

'Of course, she's on a scholarship, isn't she?' That was Ginny, snatching at any straw to explain the inexplicable. 'Miss Eldon probably told him to get her into the book so's she'll be able to keep going when her scholarship money runs out. Very kind of her, no doubt, but not quite fair on the rest of us.'

'I don't think you do get paid for that sort of thing,' said Jessamy. 'You just get free photographs.'

'How do you know?' said Lorraine.

'Thinks she knows everything,' sneered Ginny.

Jessamy didn't think she knew everything – in fact she knew she *didn't* know everything: Mr Underdown had just marked her 0 out of 10 for her algebra homework – and in some ways she was every bit as puzzled as Ginny. Mum always said that 'Having your photograph taken isn't just a passive thing. It's no good standing there and expecting the photographer to do all the work. You have to be prepared to put something into it.'

Jessamy and Ginny were both prepared. Jessamy loved cameras, and cameras, as a rule, loved Jessamy. And Ginny without any doubt was quite striking to look at, with her greeny-blue eyes and frothing mass of deep red hair. Karen simply wasn't the sort to draw attention to herself. She was dainty and prettyish, but no one could have called her striking. She was too small and neat for that. Yet the photographer had obviously seen something in her, and Ginny might just as well face the fact that whatever it was it appealed more than green eyes and red hair and a dashing manner. Photographers were artists, of a sort, and sometimes did tend to see things that other people missed.

The Ice Maidens were chosen for the Company's Christmas show, and needless to say none of the second years was amongst them. Jessamy hadn't really expected it, so she wasn't disappointed – just meanly and sneakily glad that neither Ginny nor Lorraine had been picked.

In class they were learning the dances from Madam's own version of *A Midsummer Night's Dream* for performance at the end of term.

'Shall we go and watch the Company do it?' suggested Jessamy to Karen. 'It's on next week ... Saul's dancing Demetrius. Shall we go?'

They went on Saturday evening (because someone else, some inferior being, was dancing in the matinée) and had to queue for over an hour to get two mouldy horrible seats up in the gods on either side of a pillar. Jessamy was more used to sitting in the dress circle, or even in a box if she was with Mum and Dad, but she supposed that it was good for her, occasionally, to see things from a different perspective. After all, it was important for a dancer to know what all the various sections of the audience were experiencing. Not a great deal from up here, thought Jessamy, crossly. It was as well she had brought Mum's opera glasses. (She bet every time she handed them to Karen, Karen had them trained on Saul's face.)

Demetrius was one of Saul's best parts – romantic, passionate, but sending himself up just enough to have the audience laughing. He enjoyed playing the comedian on stage; he always complained that he wasn't allowed to be funny as often as he would have liked. (He had once informed Jessamy that his real burning ambition was to dance one of the Ugly Sisters in *Cinderella*. She *thought* he had only been joking, though sometimes with Saul it was difficult to tell. Karen, when Jessamy told her, had cried, 'Oh, no!' and for once even Jessamy was forced to agree. For Saul to dress up as an Ugly Sister would be the most terrible waste.)

'Which bit do you hope you're picked for?' said Jessamy, as the curtain came down at the end.

'Oh, one of the Fairies!'

'Which one?'

'Mm . . . don't really mind. I bet they choose you to be Puck! You'd be brilliant as Puck.'

Yes, thought Jessamy; I would. Puck was her sort of part. People who hadn't seen the ballet before always thought it was being danced by a boy until he went on point, and then they were thrown into confusion and couldn't make up their minds whether it was a boy or a girl. Jessamy would love to dance Puck.

'What I *don't* want is one of those mingy peasant dances.'

'Oh, Jessamy, they're fun!'

'They're not, they're all jolly and clumping.'

'Well, they're supposed to be. They're rustics.'

'I hate them. They're horrible.' Six soppy peasant girls in soppy blue peasant costumes cavorting about the stage with Bottom and Peter Quince and all the rest.

'The pas de deux would be all right.'

'No, it wouldn't; it would be horrible. I want to be Puck.' And if she couldn't be Puck then she'd be a Fairy. The Fairies had more real dancing to do than the soppy peasants.

'Let's go round and see Saul. Come on!'

Karen hung back. 'You go. I'll wait out front for you.'

'Oh, don't be so silly! Why don't you want to come?'

She did want to come, of course; she was just too shy. Imagine being shy of Saul! It was because she had this great sloppy thing about him. If Jessamy had had a great sloppy thing about anyone – she had once thought that she had about Sandro Corelli, but it hadn't lasted – she would seize every opportunity to go and be near them, breathing the same air, sharing the same space. It wouldn't bother her that she might be making a nuisance of herself, or that they might not want her there. If you were in the public gaze, as Saul was, it was part of the price you paid; and quite honestly she didn't think Saul minded. He was far nicer natured than the rest of the family. Dad was impatient (Jessamy took after him) and Mum could freeze faster than an iceberg if she thought someone was encroaching, but Saul had no side for all he was the darling of the London ballet scene.

'He likes to see his fans,' said Jessamy, but Karen wouldn't budge. She really would have to learn to be a bit more assertive, thought Jessamy, marching off backstage and leaving Karen to look at the photographs in the foyer. No one was going to take any notice of a shrinking violet.

Saul's dressing room was full of people, all gushing and shrieking and vying for attention. Perhaps it was just as well Karen hadn't come; she would only have hovered by the door and blushed. Jessamy, never one to lack confidence, simply put her head down and burrowed a passage through to the centre. Once there she threw her arms round Saul's neck, planted a smacking kiss on his cheeks and cried, in as theatrical a voice as she could manage, 'Daahling, you were *maaaah*vellous!' Some people laughed; some didn't. Saul only groaned and said, 'You again! Where's your little blond friend?'

'Karen? She's waiting in the foyer. She's too shy to come and see you.'

'I wish you were too shy! But did you like the show? Seriously?'

'Seriously, I did,' said Jessamy. 'Specially my lovely brother.'

'Flattery, lady, will get you nowhere. What are you after?'

'Nothing! Unless you want to give us a lift home.'

'On your bike!' said Saul. 'What do you think I am, a public hire service?'

'It's all right,' said Jessamy. 'Sid's coming for us.' Sid was Belinda Tarrant's own private cab driver. If he couldn't manage to come himself, he always sent 'one of my lads'.

'Actually I wasn't after anything,' said Jessamy. 'I thought you were brilliant, gorgeous, stunning and delectable.'

'I am gobsmacked,' said Saul. He gave her a little push. 'Go and get your cab and don't keep Sid waiting.'

As Jessamy pushed her way back out, a boy with a shock of sandy hair and a face like an amiable cart horse smiled at her and held open the door.

'You must be Jessamy,' he said.

'That's right.' Jessamy stopped and bestowed a large beam upon him. It was always pleasant to be recognized.

'I'm Ken.' He held out a hand. Jessamy took it, graciously.

'How do you do?' she said, in her best Belinda Tarrant manner. She would have liked to stay and talk to him and find out what he was – certainly not a dancer: far too large and gangling – but Karen would be worried if she stayed away too long and Mum would be cross if they kept Sid hanging about.

As it happened, Karen was herself engaged in conversation. It was most extraordinary, because Karen never talked to strangers, especially not strange men. What was even more extraordinary –

Jessamy plunged across the foyer, arriving just as the man was taking his leave.

'Well, if it isn't young Jessamy!' he said. He nodded at her. 'Your brother gave a first-rate performance tonight.'

'Do you know who that was?' demanded Jessamy, as she and Karen made their way to the exit.

'No. He just came up and started talking to me.'

'It was Eric Lauder!'

Karen looked at her, horrified. 'The ballet critic?'

'Yes! What was he saying to you?'

Karen, predictably, blushed. 'He said, "That's a very nice line you've got there, my dear." '

'Why?' Jessamy looked at her, sharply. 'What were you doing?'

Karen's blush deepened. 'I was looking at a photo of Colleen McBride in *Giselle*, and I – '

'You what?'

'I sort of . . . started copying her.'

'In *public*?' Jessamy was genuinely shocked. It was one thing to dance about on a tube train; quite another to do it in the foyer of the Fountain Theatre in front of half the glitterati of the London ballet world. 'Talk about shameless!' said Jessamy.

'I didn't realize I was doing it,' whispered Karen.

'No, you got carried away. Well, it's very bad manners,' scolded Jessamy. 'It's like – like going up the road in full costume and make-up between performances.' It was something you just didn't *do*. And to be caught at it by Eric Lauder, of all people!

'I suppose he didn't ask who you were?' said Jessamy.

Karen stared at her, wide-eyed and frightened. 'Yes, he did! He wanted to know where I was studying. You don't think he's going to complain to Madam about me, do you?'

'Serve you right if he did,' grumbled Jessamy; but of course he wouldn't. More likely, one of these days, there would be a glowing review of one of Karen's performances written up in the Sunday newspaper, with Eric Lauder recalling how he had 'first seen her, serenely unselfconscious, posed *en arabesque* in the foyer of the Fountain Theatre . . .'

Karen seemed possessed of an uncanny knack, thought Jessamy, of directing attention to herself without even being aware that she was doing it.

The lists went up for the end-of-term performances. Karen was Mustard Seed, and Nella was Moth. Lorraine was the 'over hill over dale' Fairy. Ginny was Titania, which everybody had expected. Maggot was Puck, which nobody had expected – least of all Maggot herself.

'Honestly, I never *dreamt*,' she kept saying, until Jessamy thought that she would scream.

Jessamy was dancing 'a guest at the wedding' and the peasant pas de deux with Karen. Guest at the Wedding was a mere nothing; just drifting about stage being stately. Karen, trying to repair her wounded pride by pointing out that dancing the peasant pas de deux wasn't like just being *a* peasant, 'soloists get to do the peasant pas de deux', only managed to make matters worse; for if soloists danced it, that meant Karen had two solo roles and Jessamy only had one.

'Fairies aren't solos,' said Karen.

Maybe not, thought Jessamy, strictly speaking; but they were named parts, and each Fairy had her own small variation to dance. Being part of the peasant pas de deux wasn't truthfully so very much better than simply being 'a peasant'. The Fairies' choreography was really inventive: the peasant pas de deux was dead ordinary in comparison. And soloists *didn't* dance it; not real soloists. Only sub-sub-soloists waiting for promotion.

'I'd sooner be a Fairy,' said Jessamy.

'The trouble is,' explained Karen, 'you don't really *look* like a Fairy.'

'So what do I look like? A peasant?'

'You look ... too *healthy*,' said Karen, choosing her words with care.

Too down-to-earth, thought Jessamy, glumly.

'You really ought to dance one of the Lovers,' said Karen; but what was the good of saying that when they weren't doing the Lovers' sequences?

Jessamy left it as long as she could before breaking the news to Belinda Tarrant.

'Peasant pas de deux?' said her mum, totally ignoring Guest at the Wedding, as Jessamy had known that she would. Guest at the Wedding was nothing. It was rubbish. 'I'd have hoped you'd do better than that!'

'Well, but I don't really look like a Fairy,' said Jessamy, 'do I?'

'No.' Her mum studied her, critically. 'I hope you're

not going to get *fat*. I think we'd better start watching your diet, my girl!'

It was all she needed. Yoghurt and raw carrots for the rest of term ... yuck!

Belinda Tarrant didn't come to the end-of-term performance, which as it happened was just as well. She would have come, had Jessamy wanted. She said, 'Would you like me to be there? I will, of course, if you think it's worth it.'

But it wasn't; not just for a mouldy old Wedding Guest and stupid peasant pas de deux.

In fact the peasant pas de deux wasn't so bad; at least it was real dancing even if there wasn't much of it. It was as a Wedding Guest that Jessamy came to grief. It was *unbearable* being on stage and having nothing to do whilst others danced. She had to find some way of livening up the performance!

She found a way: she would be a Wedding Guest who flirted. She bet people did flirt when they went to weddings! They didn't just drift about being graceful.

To begin with, Jessamy tried flirting with John McDonald, but John was too serious-minded: he only frowned at her.

Next she tried with Nicky Scott. Nicky was far more responsive. Between them, he and Jessamy were very soon providing their own comic turn at the back of the stage. Jessamy began it by peering coyly round the edge of her fan: Nicky promptly responded with a lecherous leer. Jessamy tapped his wrist: Nicky blew her a kiss. Jessamy stamped on his toe: Nicky hopped in agony.

People all about them were convulsed in silent fits of the giggles.

Miss Eldon was furious afterwards. She took Jessamy and Nicky to one side and said that if either of them ever behaved so disgracefully on stage again she would refuse to have them in her class.

'You can think yourselves lucky that Madam wasn't here. You can also think yourselves lucky that I'm not going to report you. But I give you due warning – you especially, Jessamy! Someone with your background . . . I really would have expected you to know better. You ought to be thoroughly ashamed of yourselves! There is simply no excuse for bad manners on stage.'

What a way to end the term! Looking back on it, thought Jessamy, it had been absolutely beastly from start to finish.

5

'Stop!'

Belinda Tarrant's voice rang out, sharply. The class froze; even Jessamy froze. Jessamy was actually more in awe of her mum than she was of Madam.

'Might I ask you, Jessamy – ' Belinda Tarrant fixed her daughter with a steely grey-eyed gaze – 'whether you consider yourself to be one of us or whether you are merely gracing us with your bodily presence whilst your mind roams elsewhere?'

For once, Jessamy's normally pink cheeks achieved a touch of hot tomato. Mum could be so horribly sarcastic!

'I put the question,' said Belinda Tarrant, 'since I observe no signs of actual life in you. Are you with us, or have you perhaps become too grand to mix with ordinary mortals?'

'With you,' muttered Jessamy.

'Then kindly pull yourself together and put some effort into it!'

Nobody sniggered because nobody would dare, but Jessamy bet there were some who would have liked to. She glared angrily ahead as she resumed her position at the barre. Selma, with her fat rice pudding thighs, was directly in front of her, Dawn Collier wobbling about behind. It wasn't right that she and Karen should have to come back and join in with all the old crowd again just because it was holidays. If Mum insisted they take class, then she ought to let them do it in private. Karen and Jessamy were full-time ballet students! They shouldn't be expected to work with *amateurs*.

Of course, Mum had it in for Jessamy just at the moment; it was her school report that had done it. School reports had never in the past caused Jessamy any particular anxiety. She had simply handed them over to Mum and forgotten about them. Sometimes, she suspected, neither Mum nor Dad had even bothered to read them, so if teachers had complained about Jessamy's inability to master the complexities of long division or her lack of attention in chemistry classes – which they almost certainly *would* have complained about – Mum and Dad would never have known, and probably wouldn't have cared even if they had. At any rate, they had never said anything to Jessamy. So long as she worked at her dancing, that was all that mattered.

Unfortunately, the report that had been sent from ballet school had complained about other things besides stupidity over long division and non-attention in chemistry classes – and this time, Mum and Dad *had* read it. Both of them. But it was Mum, as usual, who had spoken to her.

'Jessamy, I'm not at all pleased with this report! I think you'd better take a look at it.'

Jessamy had looked, and to begin with couldn't see what her mum was complaining of.

Lower School Report

Name: Jessamy Hart   Class: Miss Eldon's

Classical Ballet

Batterie	Good strength in feet and ankles. Excellent precision.
Elevation	Has natural high jump. Must work to control landings.
Pirouettes	Instinctive feel for turn and speed. Good control. Needs to work on fouettés.
Point Work	Good speed and precision but must not become complacent.
Ports de bras	Needs to improve placing. A tendency to strain hands and neck.
Adagio	Must work hard to improve steadiness.

All right, the last two could have been a bit better, but no one was perfect at *everything*. What did Mum expect?

'Read the General Remarks.' Mum had said it grimly. 'That's the bit that bothers me.'

Jessamy had let her eye speed further down the page.

General Remarks

Jessamy is without any doubt a most assured young dancer with a strong technique and good potential. She needs to work hard at controlling the flow of her movement and pay special attention to her hands and feet. At the moment she is still a little tense.

So?

'Go on,' had said Mum.

If there is one area which gives us cause for concern it is her general attitude towards her studies. She has yet to convince us that she has the necessary determination and single-mindedness to complete the course. We hope that she will prove us wrong, but we shall need to see a change in attitude during the coming term.

Jessamy had read it with growing dismay – not unmixed, it had to be said, with a slight edge of resentment. Who was Miss Eldon to say what her attitude was? Only Jessamy knew that.

She had said as much, defensively, to her mum, but Belinda Tarrant had retorted crossly that 'It's obviously the impression that you give. Now I know why you weren't trusted with anything better in the end-of-term performances! They're not going to give the best parts to people who have the wrong attitude.'

It was then she had decided that both Jessamy and Karen should come back to the Tarrant Academy and have classes during the Christmas holidays. It wasn't the classes that Jessamy minded – well, not so much; it was having to take them with all those people she thought she had left behind. Selma and Dawn and the rest. She was sure her mum was only doing it because she thought Jessamy needed cutting down to size.

She had tried grumbling to Karen about it, but Karen was never a very satisfactory person to grumble to. She either sympathized too much, so that you began to feel patronized and wished you hadn't said anything, or else she saw the other person's point of view and was earnestly – and maddeningly – reasonable. On this question of ballet classes, she was earnestly and maddeningly reasonable.

'I don't really see that it's all that different from Company class... I mean, people like Saul' (hot tomato and sizzling fried eggs) 'people like Saul have to stand at the barre next to members of the corps de ballet ... it's just the same sort of thing.'

'It's not the same sort of thing! At least they are all *professionals*.'

'Yes, but we're not,' said Karen.

'We are almost.'

'Well, I still don't see why it bothers you.'

Karen wouldn't; she was so *humble*.

Just before Christmas, Jessamy met up with her two best friends from Coombe Hurst, Sheela Shah and Susan Garibaldi. They all went into the Burger Hut to eat beanburgers and French fries – including Jessamy, in a spirit of defiance. She was never allowed French fries at home, while in the CBS canteen they were quite simply unheard of. For all that the skinbags in Miss Eldon's class were aware, such a delicious item of food might never have been invented.

'You'll cop it,' said Sheela, 'next time you get on the scales.'

'Not going to get on any scales,' said Jessamy. Not until the beginning of term, and by then she would have worked it all off.

It was strange, being in the company of ordinary people again – people whose lives weren't bounded by the speed of their pirouettes or the line of their arabesques. It wasn't any use talking to Susan and Sheela about ballet school for it would have meant nothing to them – all the little anecdotes such as Maggot thinking Madam wanted them to do pliés fast, and Lorraine trying to give herself these fantastic false insteps by using dozens of layers of sticking plaster, which had all fallen off the first time she had gone on point. They would have listened politely, but they wouldn't really have understood. (Why *shouldn't* you do pliés fast? And what were false insteps, and why would anyone want them?)

On the other hand, Jessamy could listen quite happily to tales of Coombe Hurst – how they had Miss Roper as class teacher and how she was *foul*, and how Mrs Truelove, who had been their class teacher in Year 7, had left to have a baby and the baby had turned out to be triplets and Mrs Truelove had brought them into school so that people could see them.

Now that she had left, Jessamy wasn't specially interested in Miss Roper being foul, and she wasn't interested in babies at the best of times, and specially not three all together (all those dirty nappies! Ugh! Horrible!) but it was fun to be with Susan and Sheela again. She enjoyed listening to their burble, even if she did feel curiously distant from it. One thing was certain: she could never go back to an ordinary school again.

'Hey! Guess what?' said Susan, suddenly tapping Jessamy self-importantly on the back of the hand.

'What?'

'We've started riding!'

'Horse riding?'

'Yes, it's brilliant, we're going for a special ride on Boxing Day. Want to come?'

'I can't ride,' said Jessamy.

'Nor can we, properly. She – ' Susan jerked a thumb at Sheela – 'fell off at the walk the other day.'

'Yes, and she – ' not to be outdone, Sheela jerked a thumb at Susan – 'couldn't get her horse to move at all.'

'But it's brilliant,' said Susan. 'Why don't you come?'

Jessamy was tempted. She had always had a hankering to go horse riding. Of course, she knew what her mum would say: horse riding develops the wrong muscles. But just going *once* couldn't hurt, could it?

'Ask if you can,' said Sheela.

'I'll ask,' said Jessamy, 'but I'll bet she'll say no. She always says no to anything like that.' Tennis, hockey, horse riding . . . swimming was the only form of sport that Belinda Tarrant really considered acceptable.

'You do have to lead the most awfully sheltered existence,' said Susan. 'Anyone would think you had one of those weird illnesses where you have to live in a bubble.'

'It's a bit like that in some ways.' Jessamy said it rather gloomily. Couldn't eat what you wanted, couldn't do what you wanted, couldn't wear what you wanted, couldn't cut your hair how you wanted –

'I think you must be loopy,' said Sheela, 'to put up with it.'

'So do I, sometimes,' agreed Jessamy. 'But it's the price you pay.'

'For *what*?' said Sheela. 'By the time you're thirty you'll be all old and knackered and past it.'

'People are at thirty anyway,' said Jessamy.

'Not everyone. Not politicians aren't.'

'So who wants to be a politician?'

'Who wants to live in a *bubble*?'

They didn't understand, and it wasn't the least use trying to explain. They had never experienced the heady magic of being on stage, or the thrill of finally conquering a new sequence of steps, or the sense of satisfaction it gave to be in command of your body and know that you could make it do whatever you asked of it.

'I'll see what she says,' said Jessamy. 'Perhaps as it's Christmas she might let me.'

'Absolutely not,' was what Belinda Tarrant said, just as Jessamy had known that she would. 'You'll develop the wrong muscles and look like some ghastly coal heaver.'

'But it's only once!' pleaded Jessamy. Just going once couldn't make her look like a coal heaver. 'And it is Christmas!'

'Yes, and you could still fall off and break something.'

'But we're only going to *walk*.'

'In that case, you might just as well walk on your own two feet. I'm sorry, Jessamy; you know the rules.'

'But it's not fair! I'm never allowed to do anything!' cried Jessamy.

Belinda Tarrant turned, and looked at her; one of her cold, considering looks.

'It is exactly this sort of attitude,' she said, 'that Miss Eldon is complaining of. You either want to be at ballet school, or you don't. If you don't, then say so immediately and we'll send you back to Coombe Hurst.'

65

Jessamy pursed her lips, rebelliously. 'I do,' she said, 'but I still don't think once could have hurt.'

Christmas Day arrived, and with it the usual flood of ballet books and ballet videos and multi-coloured pairs of leg warmers and crossovers. Karen – whom she couldn't see on Christmas Day because of Karen having to stay and keep her gran company – had given her a brooch in the shape of a ballerina: Jessamy had given Karen a framed print of ballet dancers. Jacquetta came, with the baby and the Bottler (the Bottler was her husband: his real name was Brian). Jacquetta's present was a basket of soaps and perfumes from the Body Shop. Hooray! thought Jessamy. A *normal* present for once.

Half way through the morning, unexpectedly, Saul turned up.

'You again!' said Jessamy.

'Don't worry about her,' said Saul, to the friend he had brought with him. (It was the boy with the nice horsey face, whom she had met in Saul's dressing room.) 'It's only something the cat sicked up.'

'We haven't got a cat!' said Jessamy. 'And why,' she added, in aggrieved tones, 'didn't anyone tell me that you were coming?'

'Because people don't necessarily tell you every-thing?' suggested Saul.

'People don't tell me *anything*,' grumbled Jessamy. 'Him and Mum – ' she addressed herself to the boy with the horsey face, whose name she now remembered was Ken – 'they do nothing but have secrets together and they never let me in on them.'

Ken raised a sympathetic eyebrow.

'It's very bad manners,' said Jessamy, 'isn't it?'

'Very bad manners to think you have any *right* to be in on other people's secrets,' said Saul.

'Well, but she could at least have told me you were coming!'

'Why? Would you have bought me a present?'

'I've bought you one anyway.' Jessamy said it scornfully. 'I always do.'

'I hope it's something nice,' said Saul.

'It is, it's lovely.' It was a special polished stone from the aromatherapy shop that was for calming you down in moments of stress. All you had to do was just hold it in the palm of your hand for a few seconds and all feelings of anxiety would slip away. Jessamy had visions of Saul standing in the wings, clutching his special stone to ward off stage fright. If Saul ever had stage fright; Jessamy didn't.

She was on the point of asking him when she remembered her grievance: 'You'd think someone could just tell you when your own brother was coming home!'

'You would, wouldn't you?' agreed Saul.

'So why didn't they?'

He pressed the tip of his finger against her nose, squashing it almost flat.

''Cause nobody knew, that's why! Even we didn't know. It was something we decided on the spur of the moment. We thought we'd look in and say happy Christmas... happy Christmas! This is Ken, by the way. Ken, this is my spoiled little sister, Jessamy.'

'We have already met.' Jessamy said it grandly. 'And I'm not spoiled, I'm not allowed to do *anything* I want.'

'Since when?'

'Since *always*!'

'So what did you want to do?'

'I wanted to go riding,' said Jessamy, 'just *once*, 'cause it's Christmas, and she won't let me.'

'Oh, now, come on!' said Saul. 'Be reasonable! We all have to make sacrifices. If you want to be a dancer –'

'Maybe I don't,' muttered Jessamy.

'Rubbish! Of course you do.'

'How do you know?'

'I know because I've seen you dance and because I know you.'

'Then you know more than I do,' retorted Jessamy.

'That,' said Saul, 'is very likely. Just live through it, kiddo! It'll pass. We've all had 'em ... periods of doubt and despondency.'

'What, even you?' said Jessamy.

'Even me, my child.'

Jessamy would have liked to believe him, but she wasn't at all sure that she did.

On Boxing Day they all went to the ballet to see Saul dance the Prince of the Four Seasons in the Christmas show. Karen wasn't able to go with them as Jacquetta and the Bottler were going, and Saul's friend Ken, and there wasn't room in the box, which Jessamy thought was a bit stingy. After all, it was far more important for Karen to watch ballet than it was for Jack, who had given it all up. As for the Bottler, he didn't even *like* it. And why should a friend of Saul's be invited and not a friend of Jessamy's? Ken wasn't a dancer; what did he want to go for?

'I should have thought that was pretty obvious,' said Jacquetta.

It wasn't obvious to Jessamy.

'Karen would have *loved* to come. She's got this thing about Saul.'

'So's Ken,' said Jacquetta; and laughed.

Jessamy looked at her, frowning. 'How do you know?'

'A little bird told me.'

Stupid, thought Jessamy. There were times when her older sister was just *stupid*.

'Actually,' said Jacquetta, 'if you want to know, he's an artist and he's making sketches of dancers for his next exhibition. Does that satisfy you?'

Not really, thought Jessamy. Why couldn't he go and stand in the wings and make sketches from there? It would be far better, and he was bound to get permission if he were a friend of Saul's. Madam would do anything for Saul; he was one of her favourites.

'Stop sulking!' said Jacquetta. 'He is *Saul's* friend, and Saul is dancing. It's only natural he should want to watch him.'

He could have done it just as well from the wings, thought Jessamy.

After the show – with Ken busy sketching by the light of a torch: *very* offputting – they all went out for supper to a 'little place' chosen by Belinda Tarrant. Jessamy's mum knew lots of little places; she usually knew the chef and the head waiter, as well. During the meal Saul passed round Ken's sketch books so that they could see all the sketches he had made. There were loads and loads of Saul, and hardly any of anybody else.

'Do you do women as well?' said Jessamy.

Jacquetta rolled her eyes. Mum said, '*Jessamy*.'

'What?' said Jessamy. She'd asked a perfectly ordinary question: she just wanted to know if he did women as well as men.

'Only if he can find one as pretty as me,' said Saul, smirking.

'You're not *pretty*.' Jessamy said it witheringly. 'Women are *pretty*.'

'Actually I'm going to do the whole company,' said Ken, 'when I can get around to it. I just started with Saul because he happened to be there.'

'Oh, is *that* the reason?' said Saul.

'I wish he'd paint me,' said Jessamy, on the way home in the Bottler's car, afterwards. 'Do you think he would, if I asked him?'

'Why should he?' said Jacquetta.

Well, thought Jessamy, everyone says I look like Saul. If he enjoyed doing Saul, why shouldn't he enjoy doing her? It would be brilliant to have someone do a real proper painting of her; loads better than a mouldy photograph.

'I think I'll ask him,' she said.

'Where are this child's manners?' demanded her dad, at the same time as Belinda Tarrant said sharply, 'You will do no such thing!'

'Why not?' Jessamy was hurt. Everyone seemed to be getting at her just lately.

'It would be very pushy,' said her mum. 'The poor boy might feel that he had to.'

'No, he wouldn't! I'd only *ask* him.'

Her dad leaned forward. 'You do not *ask* people to paint you: you wait to *be* asked.'

'Unless, of course,' said Jack, 'you're willing to pay for the privilege.'

6

'Did you have a good report?' said Maggot, as the four of them, Maggot, Nella, Jessamy and Karen, met up at Waterloo on the first day of the spring term.

'Mm . . . OK,' said Jessamy. 'What was yours like?'

'Margaret works *hard*,' said Maggot. 'She is a *determined* little dancer . . . whatever that means.'

Nella sighed. 'I need to work for strength . . . *needs strength in feet and ankles: needs strength in back*. I have *natural talent*,' said Nella, 'but I must *work to strength*.'

'Better go and join the boys in weight lifting,' giggled Maggot. 'Oh, look, there's Angie! Hey! Angie!'

Maggot went pelting off up the road and the subject of reports was forgotten. Karen wouldn't have volunteered to say what had been in hers, in any case; it would have seemed like boasting.

Karen has made extraordinary progress during her first term with us, Miss Eldon had written. *Late starter though she was, she has not only made up lost ground but has actually pulled ahead. Her dancing is fluid, her technique always precise and co-ordinated. She needs to gain strength, but is working at it.*

And then, as if that were not enough: *Karen has a shy and modest personality and shows great charm in*

*her dancing. This charm will mature as she herself grows
in confidence. An excellent term's work!*

'I suppose yours was all right?' said Jessamy, as an
afterthought, as they turned down Lower Marsh
towards Edridge Street.

'My what?' said Karen.

'Your report!'

'Oh. Yes,' said Karen. 'It was OK.'

At the usual beginning-of-term medical examination
Jessamy was found, horror of horrors, to have gained
five pounds during the Christmas holidays.

'Really, Jessamy!' scolded Miss Eldon. 'I know it was
Christmas, but you simply can't afford to binge on
chocolates and Christmas pudding. You've got a big
enough tail as it is, my girl! You don't want it getting
any bigger.'

Ginny and Lorraine, needless to say, considered it
highly amusing.

If Mum had let me go riding, thought Jessamy, I
wouldn't have felt any need to binge. There was such
a thing as *comfort* eating; hadn't Miss Eldon ever heard
of it? Some people ate because they were unhappy,
others ate because they were frustrated. You can't do
this, you can't do that . . . surely it was only natural to
rebel from time to time?

'Now, I don't want you going to the other extreme
and starving yourself,' said Miss Eldon, 'but by the end
of the month, if not before, I want you back to normal.
Or else!'

Yoghurt and raw carrot, thought Jessamy. It was all
so incredibly boring.

Two weeks after term began, Karen, alone of the

second years, was promoted to become one of Madam's 'once-a-week' specials (also known as 'Madam's faves'). The specials were a select group of mainly third and fourth years who were accorded the privilege of regular one-hour classes with Madam herself.

The news was given to Karen by Miss Eldon: she scarcely knew how to break it to Jessamy. If only they could both have been chosen! She felt almost guilty, being one of Madam's specials without Jessamy.

'I expect it's because I'm classical more than charac-ter,' she said. 'You're lucky: you're *dramatic*. Like Lynn Seymour. You're not just a dancer, you're an actress as well.'

'Yes, I couldn't bear to be just a dancer,' agreed Jessamy. 'I want to branch out and do a bit of everything . . . films, musicals, straight theatre. I don't just want to spend my life dancing.'

'Well, this is it,' said Karen. 'Dancing's all I *can* do. You'll still be able to work when I'm forced to retire.'

'Ballet is so limiting,' said Jessamy.

They were brave words; but inside herself she felt the first icy fingertips of panic. She had come back to school so full of good intentions! She was going to work really hard – she *had* worked really hard; and still Karen had been chosen instead of her. Mum wouldn't say anything, but she would purse her lips when she heard, because of course she would hear, sooner or later, and Jessamy would know that she was proving a disappointment. Jack had been a disappointment; don't say Jessamy was going to be another one?

I couldn't bear to end up as a nobody, thought Jes-samy. There had to be something she was good at –

74

outstandingly good at. Head and shoulders better than anyone else. She couldn't bear to be a nobody and she couldn't bear to be just average. Jessamy meant to go somewhere in life.

At the end of January, to make up for Karen missing out on Boxing Day, Saul got them two seats for the last Saturday afternoon performance of *The Seasons*.

'Come round afterwards,' he said, 'and maybe we'll take you out to tea.'

'Out to *tea*?' said Karen, eyes wide as satellite dishes. 'He's going to take us out to *tea*?'

'Why not?' said Jessamy. 'He's my brother.' Brothers ought to take their sisters out to tea occasionally. 'If you like,' said Jessamy, 'you can sit next to him . . . you might even be able to *touch* him.'

'Oh, Jessamy, don't!' said Karen.

The Prince of the Four Seasons was not one of Saul's favourite roles (mainly because there was no chance to be funny) any more than *The Seasons* was one of his favourite ballets. It wasn't one of Jessamy's, either, but it was always popular with Christmas audiences, many of whom knew nothing whatsoever about ballet and only came once a year for a special treat. Also, if you happened to be one of Saul's fans it gave you what Jessamy's dad had once wryly described as 'a veritable feast of visual delight'. Saul as the Prince of Spring, young and tender: as the Prince of Summer, languid and sultry: as the Prince of Autumn, energetic, athletic, covering the stage in great leaps and spins; and finally, the one Jessamy liked best, the Prince of Winter, classic and crystalline, clad in white from head to foot, dancing his love duet with the Snow Spirit (Colleen McBride) as the Ice Maidens slowly froze in the background and the snowflakes fell.

'You'll be an Ice Maiden next year,' whispered Jessamy to Karen.

'And you!' said Karen.

Jessamy shook her head. 'I won't. I'm not Madam's type.'

Karen looked at her, doubtfully. If she tells me again that she's classical and I'm dramatic, thought Jessamy, I shall scream. She knew that Karen meant well, and had only been trying to soften the blow, but really, if anything, it had just made matters worse. It made Jessamy feel that she was being patronized. Karen needn't think *she* cared about not getting into Madam's grungy old class. Ballet wasn't the only thing in life.

'OK, we're not going anywhere posh,' said Saul, when they went round afterwards (Karen hiding behind Jessamy and bright scarlet like a holly berry). 'We're going somewhere small and dark and grotty where I shan't be recognized.'

'No expense spared,' said Jessamy.

'Precisely!'

('Jessamy,' said Karen, later, 'how *could* you? It wasn't the money he was worried about. He just didn't want people bothering him.' Karen always took everything so seriously. It probably came from not having any brother of her own. She couldn't understand that despite all the jokes and insults Jessamy loved Saul almost more than she loved her mum and dad.)

Over tea, Ken showed them his sketch book.

'Look, you see, I do do women.' He had done Colleen McBride as the Snow Spirit, the Ice Maidens,

frozen like statues, Gemma Dugard in rehearsal for
Sylphides, members of the corps warming up before
class.

'Are you going to make a book of them?' said
Jessamy.

'No, I'm going to take the odd one or two and work
them up into paintings.'

'And have an exhibition?'

'I hope so.'

How wonderful, thought Jessamy, to be hung in an
exhibition for everyone to see! *Jessamy Hart, preparing
for class . . . Jessamy Hart, putting on point shoes . . .
Jessamy Hart, en attitude . . .* Why *shouldn't* she ask Ken
if he would paint her? He could always say no if he
didn't want to.

If Saul hadn't been there, she would have done so;
as it was, she wasn't quite brave enough. Saul might
tell Mum and Dad, and then they would be mad at her.
Dad could be awfully unpleasant if he thought someone
was defying him.

Going home on the tube, Karen said: 'You know
Saul's friend?'

'Ken? Yes. What about him?'

'He says he wants to paint me,' said Karen.

There was a silence. Jessamy had to struggle a long
time before she was able to say 'Really?' in a reason-
ably normal tone of voice. 'When did he say that?'

'When you and Saul were talking together about
something.'

'He said he wanted to paint you?'

'Goodness knows why,' said Karen.

'No, he'll probably do you with green hair and three

77

eyes,' said Jessamy. 'That's what modern artists usually do.'

'Who is he?' said Karen.

Jessamy knew perfectly well that when Karen said 'Who is he?' she meant 'What's his name? Is he someone I should have heard of?' She could quite easily have said, 'Kenneth Farrell. And according to the Bottler' (who surprisingly had turned out to know about art) 'he is one of the Limehouse Group and very well thought of.' Not that Jessamy had the faintest idea what the Limehouse Group was, but it sounded impressive.

Instead, in loud tones, she heard herself saying, 'He's Saul's boyfriend.'

Karen's cheeks, predictably, turned scarlet. It gave Jessamy an ignoble satisfaction. She had embarrassed her. Hah!

'Well, I don't know what you're blushing for,' said Jessamy. 'It's perfectly normal.'

'Oh, yes,' whispered Karen. 'I know.'

'Specially in the world of ballet. It's not all just pretty and tinselly; people have affairs all over the place. Mum always says it's a hotbed of intrigue and you have to be hard as nails to survive. You're so *naive*,' said Jessamy.

'I'm not!' protested Karen.

'Yes, you are. Blushing, just 'cause I told you Ken was Saul's boyfriend.'

'You mean, he isn't?'

'Well, I expect he is. In fact he almost certainly is.' It was probably what Saul had been talking about to Mum, that day they were having secrets and not letting

Jessamy in on them, as if she were still five years old and too young to know about such things.

'But I don't see that it makes any difference,' said Jessamy. 'Except, of course – ' she giggled – 'it's not much use you going all gooey-eyed over him if he's not into women.'

Heavens! Now she was blushing again.

'You know something?' said Jessamy. 'You're going to have to get your act together if you don't want to be trampled on. You are so easily shocked it is *unbelievable*.'

'I'm not shocked,' mumbled Karen.

'Well, embarrassed, then. It's the same thing. Honestly! You look like a pillar box!'

There were times when Jessamy actively disliked herself. Better to be naive and shockable than downright mean. Why do I behave like this? she thought. But she knew why: she was jealous. Being jealous of your best friend was just about as low as you could sink. Karen wasn't the only one who was going to have to get her act together; Jessamy was, too.

But I won't be a nobody! she thought. I won't!

There had to be *something* she could do better than anyone else.

7

'You *can* build up insteps,' insisted Lorraine. She was sitting on the floor of the changing room surrounded by dozens of discarded strips of sticking plaster. 'I read about someone who did it.'

'You obviously didn't read how they did it,' said Maggot.

'It didn't say how they did it; it just said they built them up with sticky plaster ... layer upon layer. It took them hours.'

'Before every performance?'

'Yes. They had to get in extra specially early.'

'Needed their brains looked at,' said Jessamy.

'It's all right for you,' retorted Lorraine. 'You've *got* insteps.'

Jessamy did a pretend faint. Lorraine? Saying something nice to her? The heavens should fall! And then she thought, perhaps she doesn't regard me as competition any more ...

Jessamy's normally buoyant confidence had undergone several knocks just recently, what with her report, and Karen being chosen to be one of Madam's specials, and Ken wanting to sketch her and not Jessamy.

'Do you remember,' said Karen, also sitting down,

to massage her feet, 'how we used to long to go on point?'

'Yes, because it didn't feel like real dancing until you could.'

'And now we have and it's agony!' moaned Nella.

'My shoes were full of blood yesterday,' said Karen.

'I just feel like I'm *crippled*,' added Nella.

'If you look at pictures of dancers' feet they're really horrible . . . all knobbly and gnarled. I suppose,' said Karen, 'that ours will get like that.'

Mine won't, thought Jessamy. Jessamy never had any trouble with her feet, just as she had never had any trouble going on point. She didn't suffer the tortures that seemed to afflict other people.

'Of course, you're probably feeling it because of your extra classes,' said Maggot, plopping down on the floor next to Karen.

'But it's only once a week!'

'Yes, but I bet she works you hard.'

'She does,' admitted Karen. 'Miss Eldon's almost like a rest cure.'

'You know why they put people in Madam's special classes, don't you?' Ginny had crouched down and was whispering, audibly, into Lorraine's ear. Lorraine looked round, uncertainly.

'They do it if they're not sure whether they're going to keep them on . . . it's a sort of last chance.'

'Who says?' demanded Maggot.

'Oh! Sorry.' Ginny straightened up. 'You weren't meant to hear.'

'Well, I did hear, and it's rubbish!' said Maggot.

Ginny shrugged. 'If that's what you choose to believe.'

'You don't want to take any notice of people like that,' said Nella, as Ginny went swishing out of the room; but it was too late, the damage had been done. Karen, being Karen, was only too humbly ready to believe that what Ginny had said might be true. She worried about it all the way home on the tube.

'It makes sense. I mean, why only pick me? I'm not that much better than anyone else. I'm obviously far *worse*!'

'Did Miss Eldon say you were far worse?'

'Well – n-no, but – '

'Don't you think she would have done?'

'Maybe she didn't want me to know.' Karen turned a distressed face to Jessamy. 'Maybe it's my last chance and she was just being kind!'

Jessamy fixed her with a stern eye. 'What did your end-of-term report say?'

Karen hesitated.

'Come on!' said Jessamy. 'What did it say?'

'It said ... an excellent term's work,' mumbled Karen.

'Well, there you are!' (I will not be jealous, thought Jessamy. I will *not*.) 'They're hardly likely to say an excellent term's work one minute and then turn round and tell you it's your last chance the next, are they? Well, *are* they? It doesn't make any sense. And besides,' said Jessamy, 'everyone knows that Madam's specials are special 'cause they're the ones she's thinking of taking into the Company.'

'Oh, but Jessamy, how could she be? It's far too early to tell!'

'Not with fourth years.'

'But I'm only second!'

'So think yourself lucky. You really must learn,' scolded Jessamy, 'to be a bit thicker skinned. Ballet is full of horrid jealous creatures like Ginny. You just have to ignore them. And why don't you try stuffing lambswool in your point shoes? It might stop your feet from bleeding.'

'Yes, I'll try it.' Karen nodded, gratefully. 'I wish my feet were like yours! Sometimes when I watch you it's like you were *born* to dance on your toes.'

It was true that Jessamy could probably claim to be better at point work than anyone else in the class. Point work was one thing at which she *was* outstanding. But it wasn't enough! There was more to ballet than point work.

Next morning they had English with Miss Lampeter. They were reading *The Merchant of Venice*; they had been reading it since the beginning of term and had reached Act IV, taking it in turns to play the various characters. So far, Jessamy had only been cast as Salarino, 'a friend of Antonio and Bassanio'. Salarino was a piddling little part. It had been very frustrating for Jessamy, with her dramatic ambitions, having to sit in silence for most of the lesson and listen whilst others murdered Shakespeare. Today, when she had almost given up hope, Miss Lampeter said, 'And let's have Jessamy as Portia.'

Portia! She was one of the leading roles. She was the one who dressed up and pretended to be a judge so

83

that she could stop Shylock exacting his pound of flesh and killing Antonio. Shylock was entitled to his pound of flesh, but what he wasn't entitled to was any of Antonio's blood. He could only have the flesh so long as he didn't take the blood as well – and of course he couldn't avoid taking the blood, so in the end he had to give up his claim and Antonio went free, which wasn't altogether fair, thought Jessamy, but then things weren't always fair in a court of law.

She listened impatiently as the two boys playing the Merchant and Shylock stumbled through their lines. Why did people read so badly? It made Jessamy clench her fists beneath her desk and mutter to herself.

At last it came to her turn, and to Portia's big speech –

The quality of mercy is not strained,
It droppeth as the gentle rain from heaven
Upon the place beneath.

Jessamy didn't, to be honest, understand everything that Portia was saying, even though they had been through the story with Miss Lampeter before embarking on the play, but she enjoyed the sound of the words and pretending to be a woman dressed up as a man and standing up in court.

She read the speech in what she thought was a suitably solemn and judgelike sort of voice. At one point she noticed Lorraine and Ginny nudging at each other and sniggering, which was a bit offputting, but had she not lectured Karen about the need to be thick-skinned and ignore people like Ginny and Lorraine? One ought to practise what one preached.

It was easier said than done, especially when you were acting as hard as you could (and not always quite sure what you were saying) but Jessamy stuck valiantly to her guns.

Miss Lampeter didn't pass any comment at the end of class. She didn't even say, 'Thank you, Jessamy,' or 'That was excellent!' though Jessamy knew she had read far better than anyone else. In the meanwhile, Ginny and Lorraine were finding it amusing to go round chanting 'The quality of mercy is not *strained*', in silly, exaggerated voices which made people laugh.

Jessamy tried not to mind, but it was very hard. She knew now how Karen must feel – except that Karen had been invited to join Madam's specials, while Miss Lampeter hadn't even said 'Well done' to Jessamy. If she could just be singled out for *something*, thought Jessamy, she wouldn't mind how much people laughed at her.

In classical mime, which they had for one hour a week, they laughed at her again, copying her gestures and making them overblown and crude, when Jessamy was putting all she could into being Odette (turned into a swan by the wicked von Rothbart) describing her plight to Prince Siegfried. Fortunately, this time, Mr Westlake put them in their place.

'Remember,' he said, 'that these gestures have to be seen by everyone in the theatre, not just those sitting in the front row of the stalls. They need to be big – they need to be expressive. It's no use making these tiny little niminy piminy movements – ' He mimicked what some people had been doing. 'They're not going to cross the footlights. Jessamy had the right idea. Big and bold, with plenty of feeling! Good! A bit more attention to detail, and you'll be fine.'

For the first time in almost longer than she could remember, Jessamy was able to bask in words of praise. Nobody else had been told they were good. Maybe mime was what she was going to shine at; mime was where she was going to be better than the rest of them.

And then she heard Mr Westlake say, 'Karen, that was excellent! It was clear, it was neat, I really can't fault you!' and her heart plummeted right down as far as her shoes. Was Karen even going to beat her at mime?

There was only one class where Karen couldn't beat her – where nobody could beat her – and that was Character. Jessamy loved Character! She loved the dazzle and the whirl and the sheer vitality of it.

They were doing a *csárdás* (Mr Badowski pronounced it 'chardash') to some bouncing Hungarian dances by a composer called Kodály (which Mr Badowski pronounced Kode-eyey). Jessamy was in a world of her own. The music fizzed and bubbled, carrying her along. One by one, as Mr Badowski silently motioned to them, the others fell out, until only Jessamy was left, a lively figure in her vivid red practice skirt and crimson shoes.

As the dance came to an end, it was greeted by a burst of spontaneous applause; even Ginny and Lorraine joined in. For almost the first time in her life, Jessamy found herself blushing.

'Thanking you, thanking you!' Mr Badowski ran forward to embrace her. 'This, you see – ' he spun round to face the rest of the class – 'this is what I look for! The fun, the excitement! All of you – you! You!' He poked first at Nella, then at Lorraine. 'Very pretty to watch, but where the passion? Where the *inner fire*?'

He dismissed them with a contemptuous wave of the hand. 'Pale imitation! Too nice – too English! Little ballet girls, always so polite, so genteel . . . for the future you must give it some stick! Yes?'

He drummed his heels, a rapid rat-tat-tat of machine gun fire on the studio floor.

'Be like Jessamy! Abandon yourselves! You, my dear, especially.' He patted Karen's cheek with a fatherly hand.

'You have much potential. Do not be too ladylike! And you – ' he turned to Ginny. 'For you is just the opposite. Also much potential. But tendency to be vulgar! Let us have inner fire, but let us also have integrity!'

Jessamy's heart bounced triumphantly all the way home. That was one in the eye for Ginny Alexander! Tendency to be vulgar! And Karen . . . what was it he had said? 'Much potential, but do not be too ladylike.'

She had never thought the day would come when she would rejoice to hear Karen being criticized. But oh, it was so good, just for once, to be better at something!

The Thing that Lived under the Stairs, wrote Jessamy, and underlined it with a firm black line.

Nobody had ever seen the thing that lived under the stairs but everybody knew that it was there. They could

*hear it snuffling and grunting in the depths of the night.
It must have been a large thing, because sometimes it
banged about and made scratching noises with what
sounded like the claws of a huge wild beast. Everybody
except Jenny was frightened of it.*

*Jenny was one of the children who lived in the house.
She was determined to find out what the thing was, and
so one night she wrapped herself in the duvet and hid
behind the telephone table with a torch, waiting for the
moment when the thing came out. Everybody, including
her big brother Sebastian and her big sister Julie, had
told her that it was wisest to leave the thing alone, but
Jenny wouldn't listen, she always thought she knew best.
She said if there was a thing in the cupboard, then the
family ought to know what it was. After all, it was their
house and it was their cupboard.*

*At the stroke of midnight the cupboard door opened
very s.l.o.w.l.y, creaking as it did so, and out trundled
this monster in the shape of the sausage vacuum cleaner
that Elke, the au pair, used for vacuuming the stairs. It
had a row of bristles down its back, rather like the
bristles on the big yard broom, and teeth as long and
sharp as garden shears, and what it did to know-it-all
Jenny no one ever discovered for when the family came
downstairs the next morning Jenny had disappeared. All
that was left was the duvet. But the funny thing was,
there now seemed to be two things in the cupboard,
scratching and snuffling and scraping with their
claws . . .*

Jessamy was proud of her story. She had written it
for English homework.

'Let's have a change from Shakespeare,' Miss Lampeter had said, because by now they had finished *The Merchant of Venice*. 'Let's all write spooky stories . . . let's see who can write the spookiest. Who's got the most vivid imagination?'

It seemed that Jessamy had. Miss Lampeter asked her to read out her story to the rest of the class, and even Ginny and Lorraine gave little screeches in all the appropriate places.

'Well, that was *really* spooky,' said Miss Lampeter. 'Perhaps when you're too old to dance any more, Jessamy, you might become a short story writer!'

Jessamy hurried home at the end of school, eager to boast of her achievement.

'Mum,' she said, 'do you want to hear a spooky story that I wrote? A *really* spooky story? It's called *The Thing that Lived under the Stairs*, and – '

'Darling, I'd love to,' said Belinda Tarrant, 'but I positively must dash, I've got a mother coming to see me.'

'Miss Lampeter said it showed a very vivid imagination!' called Jessamy, as Belinda Tarrant picked up her bag and made for the door.

'Did she? That's good! The more imagination you have, the better. I can't stand unimaginative dancers. Read me the story tomorrow!'

She didn't want to read it tomorrow, she wanted to read it *now*. She went upstairs in search of her dad.

'Dad, would you like to hear a spooky story that I wrote?'

'Some other time, Jess. I'm expecting a call from the States.'

'But, Dad, it wouldn't take a minute! It's ever so short. Look!'

As Jessamy held out the story to show him, the telephone rang. Her dad leapt at it and snatched up the receiver.

'Al? Great! Now, listen, about this idea of using Keating and Dufay – '

Carlos Keating and Antoinette Dufay; two of the stars of the Paris ballet. What was her dad planning now? Whatever it was, it was obviously more important than listening to Jessamy's potty little spooky story. Some big New York production, probably, which meant he'd be flying off again and they wouldn't see him for weeks.

Slowly, Jessamy trailed back down the stairs to the hall, and down again to the basement, which was where most of the life of the house took place. Marisol was down there, with Jacquetta's baby, known as Tork, short for Torquil. Jacquetta and the Bottler had gone gallivanting off to Switzerland, leaving Tork behind for Mum to look after – not that Mum ever did much more than cuddle him occasionally. It was left to Marisol to do all the hard work, such as feeding him and dressing him and keeping him amused. He had long since passed the nappy stage, thank goodness, and in fact really wasn't bad as two-year-olds went. Jessamy was almost quite fond of him.

She wondered if Tork would like to hear her story. It wasn't any use reading it to Marisol, because her English wasn't up to it.

'Shall I take him upstairs,' said Jessamy, as Tork came running towards her, 'and read to him?'

'Yes, please, Yessamy,' said Marisol. 'I think this is a good idea . . . a nice beddy-byes story.'

Beddy-byes? Where on earth had she picked that up from? Baby talk was revolting. Jessamy didn't believe in speaking down to children, not even if they were only two years old.

'Come along, then, Tork,' she said, holding out her hand. 'I'll read you a story that I've written.'

Jessamy and Tork curled up on the sofa together, Tork listening big-eyed with his thumb in his mouth as Jessamy read to him.

'*The Thing that Lived under the Stairs*,' read Jessamy. '*Nobody had ever seen the thing that lived under the stairs . . .*'

Tork listened, enthralled, to the very end.

'There!' said Jessamy. 'Wasn't that a good story?'

Tork nodded.

'And now,' said Jessamy, full of benevolence and the general desire to be helpful, 'we'll go and run your bath and play submarines.'

That evening, while Dad was talking to the States yet again, and Mum was relaxing in front of the television, and Jessamy was in her bedroom wrestling with geometry homework for Mr Underdown (geometry was even worse than algebra: absolutely *nonsensical*), there came a terrible screaming from the room where Tork slept.

Jessamy threw down her pen and rushed out into the corridor. Mum came running up the stairs with Marisol at her heels. Dad, from his study, yelled, 'What the devil is going on?'

It was Tork, having a nightmare. Rocked to and fro

in his grandmother's arms, he sobbed incoherently of 'things' that lived under the stairs . . . horrible 'things' like sausages with teeth.

'Jessamy,' said Belinda Tarrant, when Tork had at last been settled back into his bed and fallen asleep, 'I can't believe you were stupid enough to read a spooky story to a two-year-old?'

'I thought he'd like it,' said Jessamy.

'Would *you* have liked it when you were two years old? Yes, upon reflection – ' Belinda Tarrant said it bitterly – 'you probably would. You were that sort of child. No sensitivity whatsoever. Oh, this really is too bad! You realize you've probably scarred that little boy for life?'

Jessamy squirmed, uncomfortably. 'I didn't mean to.'

'No, I'm sure you didn't! You just don't think. I'm really very disappointed in you!'

Jessamy's story *was* a good story, everyone said that it was. But somehow all her pride in it had gone. It wasn't very clever, frightening a two-year-old; anyone could do that.

A week later, Miss Lampeter said, 'Jessamy, I'm organizing an evening of poetry reading and scenes from Shakespeare. I was wondering . . . how would you like to do that speech of Portia's for me, the quality of mercy? I was most impressed by the way you read it in class. Do you think you could learn it in time? I don't want to burden you with too much work, but it would be nice to have you do something.'

'That's all right!' beamed Jessamy. 'I learn very quickly.'

That same night she sat up into the small hours until

92

she could recite the entire speech, all twenty-two lines of it. Ballet wasn't the only thing! She could always be an actress.

8

Jessamy's report for the spring term came just one day after the Easter holidays had begun. It was either going to mean *good* holidays – or it was going to mean bad. She snatched the envelope out of Marisol's hands and went galloping up the stairs with it to her mum's bedroom.

'Mum!'

'Heavens, Jessamy! What is it? Is the house on fire?'

'It's my report,' said Jessamy. 'I thought you'd like to see it.'

'You mean, *you* want to see it. Well, at least that shows an improvement.' Belinda Tarrant switched on the bedside lamp and held out a hand. 'Last term, as I recall, you couldn't have cared less. All right! Let's have a look.'

Jessamy settled herself on the edge of the bed, peering apprehensively over her mum's shoulder as Belinda Tarrant slit the envelope with a polished fingernail and withdrew the all-important sheet of paper.

CITY BALLET SCHOOL

Lower School Report

Name: Jessamy Hart   Class: Miss Eldon's

Jessamy's eye flew rapidly down the page. Batterie – that was OK. Elevation – that was OK. Pirouettes – they were OK. Point Work – excellent. Ports de bras – not as bad as they might have been. Adagio – mmm. Well. Adage had never been her strongest point. But on the whole –

Jessamy has shown some improvement during this term. She has heeded our comments and has worked hard. We now need to see whether she is capable of sustained effort, especially in those areas where she still shows a weakness. There is a tendency to fall back on her strengths and trust to them to carry her through. But in general, a satisfactory term's work.

Jessamy let out her breath in a sigh of relief. A satisfactory term's work! Even Mum couldn't complain about that.

'Well, I suppose it could have been worse,' said Belinda Tarrant, in tones which seemed to indicate that nonetheless it could have been a great deal better.

'Character Dancing is good,' pointed out Jessamy, hopefully.

Miss Eldon didn't take them for Character: Mr Badowski took them. Jessamy had long had the feeling that Mr Badowski quite liked her.

Jessamy dances with spirit and abandon, he had written. *She has a natural feel for rhythm and flow. Her enjoyment is infectious and she is always an exciting dancer to watch.*

The pity of it was, thought Jessamy, that Character was really just a poor relation; it didn't properly count. Not with a school as classically oriented as CBS. She remembered Jacquetta once saying, rather scornfully, that telling a dancer they were good at Character was like going backstage and telling someone 'You looked lovely, darling . . . in other words, I can't think of anything to say about the performance, but the dress was pretty.'

'All right, if you want to spend your life dancing peasant pas de deux,' murmured Belinda Tarrant, going back to re-read some of the other comments.

Jessamy picked up the envelope and took out the second, not-so-important, sheet of paper: Academic Studies. Maths, French, English: geography, history . . .

General Remarks:
Jessamy does not pay nearly as much attention to her academic studies as she should. She has a good brain if she would only use it. Unfortunately, her attitude seems to be one of 'Who needs it?'

It cannot be emphasized too strongly that with employment prospects for dancers being uncertain to say the very least, and the career of a dancer being of necessity a short one, students need to seize every opportunity offered them in the sphere of general education. *Jessamy is no exception.* It is time she came to realize this.

Jessamy pulled a face. Mrs Enwright, that was; another one who had it in for her. Her and Miss Eldon. Just because her name was Hart and she came from a famous family, they seemed convinced that she considered herself a cut above all the others. *Jessamy is no exception.* She had never thought that she was an exception! But it was a fact that you couldn't concentrate on maths and geography and all the rest *and* on your dancing; you had to make a choice. And anyway, Saul had never passed an examination in his life and look at him – premier danseur with one of the leading ballet companies in the world. So sucks to Mrs Enwright!

Jessamy found it convenient to forget that Saul, just like Karen, had been one of Madam's specials almost from the word go. All she knew was that he had no more idea than the man in the moon (or Jessamy herself) what an isosceles triangle was or what had happened in 1621 (if anything). Saul knew about dancing – and about painting and music – and not very much else, and *he* had done all right.

'Hm,' said Belinda Tarrant, in thoughtful tones.

'Look!' Jessamy had just seen something else: Miss Lampeter's English report.

Jessamy has worked well this term. Her contribution to our Shakespeare evening was greatly appreciated – she has an instinctive feel for words and drama. She also wrote an outstandingly good short story, which showed great inventiveness.

'That was the one you read to Tork. Jacquetta says he still has nightmares, poor little chap.'

'Well, she shouldn't go away and leave him!' Jessamy snatched angrily at the report and stuffed it back in its envelope. 'I always said she'd make a rotten mother.'

'She's not a rotten mother, you're a rotten aunt!'

Don't care. Jessamy scowled. She was *inventive*. You'd have thought her mum would be pleased to have an inventive daughter who showed an instinctive feel for words and drama. Other mothers would be. All her rotten one could think of to say was, 'We're obviously going to have to work on your adage.'

There were times when Jessamy didn't know why she bothered to try. It just wasn't worth it.

Ginny Alexander was having a birthday party and wonder of wonders she had invited Jessamy and Karen.

'Are we going to go?' said Karen, doubtfully. She was shy at parties and didn't even like Ginny very much.

'I'm going!' said Jessamy.

It was all right for Jessamy, she was never shy.

'I don't know why she's asked us,' said Karen.

'Oh, just to swell the numbers, I expect, 'cause we happen to live near and 'cause nobody else probably wants to go.'

Karen couldn't really imagine why Jessamy should want to. Why go to the party of someone you hated? She was always saying how foul and disgusting Ginny was.

'Parties are fun,' said Jessamy. 'Doesn't matter who's giving them. I mean, we don't have to go and talk to her or anything.'

'But it's her birthday,' said Karen.

'Oh, yes, well, you have to say happy birthday and give her something, but after that you can just go and do your own thing.'

Whatever that might be, thought Karen.

'I don't think I'll go,' she said.

'Oh, but you must! If I'm going. You never know who you might meet. It's the way it's done,' said Jessamy, 'meeting people at parties.'

Karen wrinkled her nose. 'The way what's done?'

'Getting on – being successful! You've got to get used to the idea. You can't hide away under a stone all your life. If you want to get anywhere, you've got to learn to be sociable.'

'But I haven't got anything to wear,' pleaded Karen.

'I'll buy you something. I've got this dress allowance. I can put things on Mum's account at Harrod's.'

'I couldn't do that!' said Karen, shocked.

'It's not going to be you who's doing it, it's going to be me. Don't worry,' said Jessamy. 'I'll check with Mum, but she's bound to say yes. *She* knows it pays to be sociable.'

'Where is this party?' said Belinda Tarrant.

'Near Kew Gardens.'

'All right; you can get Sid to take you there and bring you back.'

'Can Karen come and stay the night?'

'Yes, if you like. I shall be away that weekend, I'm flying over to see your father, so mind you behave yourself with Marisol.'

'I always behave myself,' said Jessamy. 'Oh, and Mum! Could I buy Karen something to wear and put it on your account?'

Belinda Tarrant raised one of her beautifully arched eyebrows into her hairline.

'She hasn't anything to wear,' said Jessamy. 'She won't come if she hasn't got anything and she ought to come, oughtn't she?'

'Ought she?'

'Well, you're always saying that it pays to be sociable – '

'Only with the right people.'

'But you never know who you might meet!'

'At a thirteen-year-old's birthday party?'

'Well, you never know,' said Jessamy. 'But anyway, she's got to get used to it. Hasn't she?'

'Certainly she needs to come out of her shell a bit more.'

'So can I buy her something?'

'As long as it's nothing too expensive. I wouldn't want her grandmother seeing it and feeling she had to pay for it. Just be a bit modest for once.'

'Mum says it's all right,' announced Jessamy, when she and Karen met up the next day. 'So let's go to Harrod's and choose things!'

Karen was quite happy to go to Harrod's – 'I've never been in here before,' she whispered, as they walked through the doors – but maddeningly she refused to let Jessamy buy anything for her.

'I couldn't! My gran wouldn't ever forgive me. She'd say it was charity.'

'Oh, pooh!' said Jessamy; but Karen had her pride, and could be stubborn.

'So what are you going to wear?' demanded Jessamy.

'I'll find something,' said Karen. 'I was talking to Nella last night and she said it doesn't really matter what you wear these days . . . it's not like when we were little and everyone got all dressed up. That was awful! Everyone had proper party frocks except me. I used to have to wear my gran's petticoats cut down with bits of lace sewn on to them!'

At any other time Jessamy would have been intrigued to hear about Karen having to wear her gran's petticoats. Today she said, 'What were you doing talking to Nella?' Nella wasn't going to the party; she lived too far away.

'She rang me.' Karen sounded surprised. What was so peculiar about Nella ringing her? 'She quite often rings me,' said Karen.

'I didn't know that.' Jessamy was aggrieved. All these things that went on behind her back! 'She never rings me.'

'Doesn't she?' said Karen. 'I never ring her, 'cause of Gran's telephone bill. I'm only supposed to telephone people if it's an emergency.'

Dreadful to be poor, thought Jessamy. And specially dreadful if you were poor and obstinate. All these heavenly dresses to choose from and Karen was going to turn up looking (probably) like some waif and stray! That wouldn't do her confidence any good.

'Let's find something for you.' Karen had gone flitting over to a rack labelled Teen Time. 'This one's nice!'

'Ugh, yuck! Horrible. Put it back.'

'But it's pretty,' said Karen. 'And it would suit you.'

'Stop sounding like my mum! I wouldn't be seen dead in it. It's revolting. I loathe pinafore dresses! All little girly and twee.'

Jessamy was after something more sophisticated.

'Something like this!'

She held it up for Karen's inspection: black satin, very slinky and short. Karen eyed it, dubiously.

'I'll go and try it on,' said Jessamy.

The black satin dress was exactly what she was looking for. She pulled back the curtain of the changing room to show Karen. There was a silence.

'Well?' said Jessamy.

'There's not much of it,' said Karen.

'Of course there's not much of it! It's a *mini* dress.' Exactly what was needed for a party; you always got too hot. 'What's the matter? Don't you like it?'

'It makes you look ever so much older,' said Karen.

'How old?'

'It makes you look about . . . sixteen.'

'I'll have it,' said Jessamy.

She bought a pair of black lacey tights to go with it, and some pointy black shoes with spike heels (Madam would go *mad*) and went running eagerly home to put everything on.

Belinda Tarrant cried out in horror when Jessamy paraded herself downstairs in her finery.

'Where on earth do you think you're going, dressed like that?'

'To Ginny's party,' said Jessamy.

'Oh, no, you're not, my girl! Over my dead body!'

'Why? What's wrong with it?'

'A, it's hideous, B, it's vulgar, and C, it makes you look like a street walker.'

'What's a st – '

'Never you mind! You're not setting foot outside this house in it and that's that.'

'But it'll be such a waste if I can't wear it!' wailed Jessamy.

'Put it away for when you're twenty-one. If you want

102

to go round making an exhibition of yourself then, I won't be able to stop you.'

Jessamy sulked. 'You said I could buy whatever I liked.'

'I said, be modest!'

'That was for Karen! When you said I could have a clothes allowance, you said I could buy what I wanted.'

'I didn't necessarily say that you could *wear* what you wanted.'

'Then what's the point of letting me buy things? If I'm not allowed to wear them?'

'The point was to give you a bit of freedom and teach you a bit of responsibility. So you've made a mistake! Don't worry, it happens to all of us. It's the way one learns. Either take it back and ask them to change it, or give it to Oxfam and go and buy something else. But whatever you do, you are not, I repeat *not*,' said Belinda Tarrant, 'going to a party dressed up like that!'

'It's so unfair,' grumbled Jessamy, when Saul rang later. 'First she tells me I can buy whatever I want, and then when I've bought it she says I can't wear it!'

If she was looking for sympathy – which she generally got from Saul – she was out of luck for once.

'It's probably because it makes you look a fright,' said Saul.

'It does not!' Jessamy was incensed. 'It makes me look sophisticated . . . Karen said it makes me look as if I'm about sixteen.'

'For a thirteen-year-old to go round looking like a sixteen-year-old is asking for trouble. Where's Mum?'

'She's out. Why is it asking for trouble?'

'Oh, just use a bit of common sense! When's she coming back?'

'*I* don't know; she didn't say. I'm sick of always being told I can't do things! I bet you weren't, when you were my age. I bet you were allowed to do whatever you wanted. You've always been her favourite, you – '

'Look, just shut up whingeing! It's all I ever hear from you. Tell Mum I rang.'

'*Please*,' said Jessamy. Honestly, some people had no manners at all. 'You're like a bear with a sore head,' she said, 'What's the problem?'

'There isn't any problem except that I have a sister who is a pain in the butt!'

Saul slammed the telephone down.

Getting too big for his boots, thought Jessamy. She said to her mum, when Belinda Tarrant came in: 'What's the matter with Saul? Has one of his favourite parts been taken off him?'

'I didn't know there was anything the matter with Saul, and even if there was I don't see that it's any concern of yours. Are you going to give that hideous dress to Oxfam or take it back and change it?'

'Going to keep it for when I'm old enough to do what I like,' muttered Jessamy.

Belinda Tarrant lightly shrugged a shoulder. 'Suit yourself.'

'It's not fair!' burst out Jessamy. 'You never mind what Saul does – '

'Saul is a grown man; he can do as he likes. When you are his age, you will also be able to do as you like. Until then,' said Belinda Tarrant, 'you do as I tell you. And what I am telling you at this moment is that you do not wear that dress to the party. Do I make myself clear?'

Mum could hardly have made herself any clearer – but Mum was not there on the day of the party. She had gone hopping off across the Atlantic to be with Dad. Marisol was there, and to be sure Marisol did blink rather when Jessamy appeared in the short, black slinky dress, but it was not part of Marisol's duties to tell the daughter of the house what to wear. All she said, very carefully, was: 'What time, Yessamy, do you think to come back?'

'Oh ... about one o'clock, I should think,' said Jessamy.

Sid called for her in the cab and they went round to collect Karen, who was carrying her overnight bag because of staying with Jessamy. Karen was wearing a skimpy little orange top and black leggings with trainers. She looked about ten; very dainty and demure, and no sophistication whatsoever.

There was a surprisingly large number of people at Ginny's party, though only a handful were from ballet school – John McDonald, Angie Samuels, Lorraine Hooper and of course Karen and Jessamy. Most of the others were either family (Ginny seemed to have heaps of cousins, thought Karen, enviously: Karen herself had none at all) or people from Ginny's old school. Jessamy, in her slinky black dress, was immediately surrounded. She drew people like a magnet. Karen was left stranded, which was what always happened to small, shy, insignificant nobodies.

Angie, who was also a bit of a nobody, slid up to her

and whispered, 'What on earth does Jessamy think she is wearing?'

'A dress,' said Karen.

'Well, I can see that it's a *dress* – '

'I think it makes her look very mature,' said Karen. You had to stick up for your best friend, even if you did privately consider the dress a bit of a disaster.

'I suppose mature is one way of putting it,' said Angie.

Karen didn't ask what other ways there might be. She was too acutely aware that some people – Ginny, inevitably, and Lorraine, but also a couple of girls from Ginny's old school – were looking at Jessamy and giggling.

'Jessamy's all done up like a tart,' said John McDonald.

Karen wasn't quite sure what a tart was, but once again she didn't ask. She had a feeling it might be something not very complimentary, and then she would have to remonstrate, on account of being loyal to Jessamy, and she would rather not have to do that because actually she quite liked John McDonald. He didn't tease like some of the boys, and even though he had just said that Jessamy was done up like a tart he hadn't said it nastily and he wasn't laughing at her.

'Do you think her mother knows she's dressed like that?' He sounded, if anything, rather concerned.

'I suppose she must do,' said Karen. Jessamy would surely have shown Belinda Tarrant the dress when she bought it?

'My mum would go raving berserk if my sister wore anything like that,' said John.

'Maybe your sister's younger.'

'She's twelve and a bit,' said John.

'Yes, well, Jessamy is thirteen,' said Karen. 'And you have to remember that her mum is different from other people's mums.'

'I suppose so,' said John, but she could tell that he wasn't convinced.

Rather to her surprise, Karen enjoyed Ginny's party. She didn't see much of Jessamy, for Jessamy seemed always to be the centre of attention and surrounded by a shrieking mob, but she talked to John and Angie and a girl called Pim (or was it Pin? It was difficult to hear, with all the noise) who wanted to know what it was like being at ballet school, and a boy called Valentine who was Ginny's cousin and really rather gorgeous, and older than the others, being nearly sixteen. Valentine was actually more interested in Jessamy than in Karen – he kept asking, 'Did Ginny say she was only thirteen?' as if he couldn't quite believe it – but Karen didn't mind, she was perfectly happy to talk about Jessamy. She knew that she was probably very backward and young for her age but she didn't think she was quite ready yet to have boyfriends, however gorgeous they were. Jessamy could have him and welcome – only talking of Jessamy, where was she? She seemed to have disappeared.

'Are you looking for your friend?' said Pim (or Pin). 'I think she left.'

'Left? Oh, but she can't have done!' cried Karen. 'Not without me!'

'Oh, well, maybe she was just going outside to get

herself together. One of the boys said something about her dress and she heard him, and I think it upset her.'

'Why?' Karen looked at her, anxiously. 'What did he say?'

'Something not very nice. And all the other boys sniggered. You know what boys are like,' said Pim.

As a matter of fact, Karen didn't; she didn't really know very much about boys at all. The ones at ballet school fooled around and told silly jokes and sometimes made silly remarks, or what Karen considered were silly remarks, but never anything unkind. Nothing that would upset anyone, and specially not anyone as robust as Jessamy. She was glad it wasn't John McDonald or the gorgeous Valentine who had been horrible (Valentine had been with her and John was sitting on the floor with Angie).

'Oh, poor Jessamy!' said Karen. 'I must go and find her!'

'Mind you, she was rather asking for it,' said Pim, 'dressed up like that.'

'I don't see that's any excuse for people being *nasty*,' said Karen.

She finally ran Jessamy to earth coming out of the downstairs cloakroom. Her eyes looked suspiciously bright, as if perhaps she had been crying, but being Jessamy she wasn't letting on.

'I came to look for you,' said Karen. 'Someone said she thought you'd gone.'

'I think we ought to be going,' said Jessamy. 'It's gone ten o'clock. I think I'll call Sid and ask him to pick us up.'

'All right,' said Karen. 'If you think we ought.'

It was just on half-past ten when they arrived back in Chiswick. Marisol was down in the basement watching television.

'So you come back!' she said. 'This is early. I am thinking to wait up until one o'clock is what you say.'

'Oh, that was just a joke,' said Jessamy. 'Anyway, it was a rotten sort of party. There wasn't anyone there who was interesting, was there?'

She turned to Karen for confirmation. Karen, obediently, shook her head.

'Just a waste of time, really. All you'd expect with someone like Ginny. And to think I spent money buying her a present!'

'And a new dress,' said Marisol.

'Oh, the dress isn't anything,' said Jessamy. 'I think I'll give it to Oxfam – unless you'd like it?' she said to Karen.

'No, honestly,' said Karen. 'I think Oxfam would be better.'

9

Of course Belinda Tarrant found out about the dress;
Jessamy should have known better than to let Marisol
see her wearing it. Au pairs always went and blabbed
to Mum. And of course Mum was furious, and went on
and on about Jessamy being disobedient and deceit-
ful, and ungrateful and not to be trusted, and 'You
don't deserve to have a dress allowance' and 'I shall tell
your father about this' *and* you couldn't be bothered to
work at your adage *and* you haven't been chosen for
Madam's special class *and* I'm not in the least bit surprised *and* it's all of a piece with your general attitude
and this *and* that until Jessamy felt like something that
had been chewed up and spat out and left to lie in a
damp and dismal heap on the carpet.

The rest of the week was predictably horrible. Mum
bawled at her in class in front of fat Selma and the
rest (who openly exulted, afterwards, in the changing
room), Tammy suddenly zoomed back into her life with
a triumphant card announcing – *gloatingly* – that she
was going to become an associate student of the Royal
Ballet School, the implication being that the Royal
Ballet School was vastly superior to any other school,
including City Ballet (which it most certainly was *not*);
and just to round things off Dad rang up, all the way
from America, to say, 'For heaven's sake, Jessamy! Pull

your finger out! You're not a child any more,' which was exactly the point she had been trying to prove. She *wasn't* a child and oughtn't to be expected to wear childish clothes. All right, so the black dress hadn't been quite the success she had hoped (her cheeks still fired up at the memory of those hateful boys and the things they had said) but anyone could make a mistake. Making mistakes was how you learnt.

She couldn't even moan to Karen because Karen was rushing off every day to sit for her portrait or whatever it was, and didn't have time for Jessamy. Whenever Jessamy rang her, in search of sympathy and commiseration, Karen could only burble excitedly about Ken and how he had asked her to do lots of different poses for him and finally settled on the simplest one of all, just sitting cross-legged on the floor, in her leotard and tights, and how Ken had said this, and Ken had said that, and 'he's really, really nice' and 'he gave me tea and biscuits' and 'he keeps asking me if I'm all right or if I'm getting a stiff neck or anything.'

'He ought to know that dancers can sit for *hours.*' Jessamy said it scornfully.

'Yes, well, he does, he knows loads about dancers, but he says he wants me to be comfortable because you can't capture the essence of people if they're all tense.'

'Oh! Get her!' mocked Jessamy.

Normally such a remark would have brought Karen down to earth with a thump – normally, such a remark would not have been *necessary*; but ever since Ken had started painting her she had become positively bumptious. Bumptious and egotistical and full of self-

111

important consequence. And all because of some stupid picture that would probably never get finished anyway, and even if it did who would want to buy it? *Portrait of Totally Unknown Ballet Student sitting on the floor.* Huh!

There wasn't anyone to listen to Jessamy and offer words of comfort. She tried ringing Jacquetta, but Jack was still mad at her for frightening Tork.

'I know you didn't mean to, but really Jessamy, it was so *thoughtless.*'

She tried ringing Maggot and Nella, but Maggot had gone and stubbed her big toe against a kerbstone and was too busy feeling sorry for herself – 'It's so badly bruised I can hardly *walk*!' – to have any sympathy left for Jessamy; while as for Nella, she was in Italy visiting Italian grandparents and probably being spoilt rotten and allowed to gorge pasta till it came out of her ears.

On Sunday, Jessamy couldn't stand it any more. She had to talk to someone or she would burst with all the rage and self-pity that was churning about inside her. She decided to go and see Saul. Even if he were still in a mood Ken would be there, and Ken (according to Karen) never got moods. Ken (according to Karen) was lovely. Almost a saint. Never got moods, never got cross, never sulked, never swore.

Saul ought to take a leaf out of his book, thought Jessamy, as she caught the tube to Hampstead. Saul's language was absolutely disgraceful, *and* he had started to sulk. He had been as cross as cross just lately. Being famous simply wasn't good for some people.

When I am famous, thought Jessamy – because she was going to be, one day – I shall behave exactly the same as I do now. Graciously, and with dignity. She held her head high. Someone in the family had to set an example.

Saul stumbled to the door pulling on his dressing gown. He stared down at Jessamy, bleary-eyed.

'Oh, it's you,' he said. He didn't sound exactly overjoyed.

'Did I wake you up?' said Jessamy. 'You look awful!'

'Thank you for those kind words. I suppose you'd better come in, as you're here.'

He held the door for her.

'Did you go to bed very late?' said Jessamy. 'You look as if you were at an orgy.'

'The word is pronounced orjy,' said Saul. 'Not orggy. And it wasn't an orgy, it was a perfectly normal party except that I didn't get home till gone six and what time is it now?' He peered round in search of a clock. '*Ten.* Have you never heard of a little instrument called the telephone? It comes in very handy for checking whether people are in a mood to be visited.'

'Yes, but I didn't ring you 'cause you've been so bad tempered just lately.'

'I shall be bad tempered again if you've come to whinge at me. Sit down, I'll make some coffee.'

'Coffee's very b – ' began Jessamy; but at a look from Saul she closed her mouth.

'Thank you,' said Saul. 'I can do without the lecture.'

Well, but coffee *was* bad for you, thought Jessamy; everybody said so. She pulled out a stool and perched herself on top of it.

'It's a good thing your fans can't see you,' she said. 'You look like a fungus!'

'Dear Jessamy!' Saul blew her a kiss across the kitchen table. 'You are such a comfort. What have you come for, anyway? I hope it's not to moan at me and tell me how badly treated you are.'

'Well, it was,' said Jessamy, 'but if you're feeling as ghastly as you look I suppose I better hadn't.'

'No. I think you certainly better hadn't. For crying out loud! I've never known anyone as spoilt as you!'

'You were more spoilt than I was,' said Jessamy. 'Where's Ken? I could moan at him. He'd listen.'

Saul poured boiling water into his coffee cup, thrust a glass of orange juice at Jessamy and sank down, opposite her, at the kitchen table.

'What do you want to moan for, anyway?'

''Cause everything's gone wrong.' Jessamy sighed. 'I don't think I'm ever going to be what Mum and Dad want me to be.'

'They want you to be happy.'

'No, they don't! They want me to be a dancer.'

'Are you saying it wouldn't make you happy to be a dancer?'

'Well . . . n-no; not that, exactly.'

'What, then?'

'I'm not prepared to make enough sacrifices!' cried Jessamy. 'I hate not being able to do things, and not being able to eat what I want to eat, and wear what I want to wear, and ballet being the only thing that matters. I got this really good report for English, and Mum treats it like it's just not important!'

'Is it important?' Saul considered her, gravely, over the rim of his cup. He didn't look quite so bad now he'd woken up a bit; not quite as grey. Of course it didn't help that he hadn't shaved and that his hair was all tousled. 'I mean, compared with dancing . . . suppose someone said to you, you could either pass your English exam or pass your dancing exams . . . which would you choose?'

'Oh, well, of course, I'd choose dancing,' said Jessamy.

'So it's no contest.'

'No, but suppose I got thrown out, or something?'

'Are you likely to get thrown out?'

'I don't *think* so,' said Jessamy, 'but they keep saying I have this attitude problem.'

'Yes, because you're loud and brash and over-confident and they want to cut you down to size. I know how they feel! I'd quite often like to cut you down to size myself.'

'But I can't help being me,' objected Jessamy.

'Perhaps you could try being you but a little less so.'

'But then I wouldn't *be* me!'

'So if you're going to go on being you, you'll have to put up with all the aggro you attract.'

'It's no good expecting me to be like Karen,' grumbled Jessamy.

'No; Karen is perfect CBS material. A demure little slip of a thing who can be moulded to suit Madam's requirements. To be fair, she has the potential. I should say your friend Karen is being groomed for stardom right now. You're a bit too pushy; you're bound to cross swords. Learn some humility is my advice.'

'I've got humility!'

'Really?' Saul raised an eyebrow. 'No one would ever know it!'

115

Jessamy sipped, frowning, at her orange juice. 'Were you a demure little slip of a thing?'

'No, but I had the advantage over you . . . men aren't expected to be demure little slips.'

'You mean, she didn't mind if you crossed swords! That's not fair!'

'True. But you know, I don't think I ever so much as looked at my English report all the time I was at ballet school. I was more blinkered than you – or more single-minded; whichever way you care to think of it. I guess it's a question of getting your priorities sorted out, deciding what you want from life, then going full steam ahead to get it.'

Like Karen, thought Jessamy. Demure little slip of a thing though she was, Karen had never had any doubts.

'Well, anyway, I hope that's helped,' said Saul. 'You're probably just on a downer at the moment. We all have 'em. There's not much you can do except live through them and wait to come out the other side.'

'I suppose so,' sighed Jessamy. But it would be easier, she thought, if everyone didn't seem to have it in for her – Mum, Dad, Jacquetta, Miss Eldon; all they ever did was nag.

'Truly,' said Saul, 'life is not a bed of roses – or if it is, one spends a disproportionate amount of time treading on the prickly bits.'

He escorted her back along the corridor to the lifts.

'Thank you for not bawling me out,' said Jessamy.

'My pleasure,' said Saul.

'Will you say hallo to Ken for me?' She wasn't sure that she liked the idea of Karen getting all matey with

Ken while she was left out in the cold. 'Where is he? Is he still asleep after the orgy?'

Saul spread his hands. 'Why ask me where he is? Am I my brother's keeper?'

'He's not your brother,' said Jessamy. She tended to take things rather literally. 'He's your friend.'

'Well, he's not here.' Saul said it curtly. 'Can you make your own way down? I'm going to catch up on my beauty sleep.'

That evening, Mum telephoned Jacquetta. She had taken to telephoning her every single week, almost, ever since Tork had been born, even though at the time she'd been cross as a hornet with Jack for leaving the ballet 'just to go and have babies'.

The conversation droned on, in its usual fashion – 'Did he? Bless him! Dear little man! Give him a big kiss from his Grandma.' As long as they were talking baby talk, Jessamy didn't bother to listen. Her ears only started flapping when she heard Mum say, 'Yes, unfortunately it all seems to have broken up . . . I don't know the details, he didn't tell me. I just know they're not an item any more.'

Who wasn't an item? What was an item? Did it mean that someone was no longer living with someone? Jessamy enjoyed a bit of gossip. She liked it when Mum got on the telephone to people and discussed all the affairs that were going on in the ballet world.

'I know, it's a shame,' said Mum. 'I always felt he was a good influence. Saul really needs someone to stabilize him.'

Saul? Jessamy's ears flew out on stalks.

117

'Have Ken and Saul had a quarrel?' she said, when at long last Belinda Tarrant put the receiver down.

'No business of yours,' said her mum.

'Why not?' said Jessamy. 'He's my brother.' If Jack could know about it, Jessamy didn't see any reason why she shouldn't. 'Anyway, I know they have, 'cause I went round there earlier and Ken wasn't there and Saul said he didn't know where he was and – '

'You went round there?' Belinda Tarrant drew her eyebrows together with just the faintest hint of irritation. 'I hope you weren't doing your self-pitying act? Poor-Jessamy, Mum's-having-a-go-at-me – '

'We talked.' Jessamy said it with dignity. 'We agreed that life was not a bed of roses.'

'Well, no, it's not for Saul just at the moment, so it would be rather *nice*,' said Belinda Tarrant, 'if you could leave him alone for a bit. Don't you think? If you really consider yourself to be so dreadfully ill treated, complain to your father.'

'I can't,' said Jessamy. 'He's one of the ones that ill treats me. Why does Saul need ... what you said? Stable-izing?'

'Being successful at an early age can put a lot of pressure on someone. Not everybody can cope with it.'

'Can't Saul?'

'I think he can. I hope he can. But I would be happier if his personal life were more settled. He is not as robust as you. You are what I should call indestructible.'

Which is why she keeps having a go at me, thought Jessamy. She never had a go at Saul.

On their first day back at school, Ginny came up to

Jessamy and loudly said, 'We went to the ballet last night and your brother was really off.'

Jessamy regarded her, haughtily. 'I suppose everyone is allowed an off night occasionally?'

'Yes, but people in his position shouldn't let their personal lives interfere with their performances. You have to think of your public.'

'After all, they are the ones who are paying,' said Lorraine.

It was annoying that in fact Jessamy was in full agreement. Everyone had heard tales of how performers had gone ahead and performed even though they were at death's door or had just heard that their mother had died. But loyalty to Saul forbade her saying so.

'I really haven't the faintest idea what you're on about,' she said.

'His love life,' said Ginny, and laughed and walked off.

'What did she mean?' said Karen, as soon as she and Jessamy were alone together.

'Don't ask me,' said Jessamy. It was terrible how your private life became everyone else's business – especially in a ballet company. Ballet companies were hotbeds of gossip. It was why Mum always had so much interesting tittle tattle with which to regale Jacquetta, and of course Jessamy always listened with all ears as soon as she got on to the gossip because it *was* interesting, knowing what people were up to that you'd heard of or seen dancing. But somehow it wasn't quite so funny when it was Ginny Alexander being snide about Saul.

'I wonder what he was dancing?' said Karen.

'*Giselle*. He's on again on Saturday. Do you want to go?'

Karen, still in the throes of passion, never needed a second invitation to go and watch Saul dance. Jessamy had a rather different motive. She couldn't *believe* that her own brother would let his personal life interfere with his performance. It just wasn't professional; and if there was one thing Saul was, it was professional down to his fingertips.

It turned out that Mum was also going to see *Giselle* on Saturday evening – 'I was going to ask if you two girls wanted to come' – as a result of which they were able to sit in comfort in the front row of the circle, rather than being stuck up in the gods, peering round pillars.

Colleen McBride was dancing Giselle. Sparks always flew when she and Saul partnered each other. Most times it made for an electrifying performance, keeping an audience on the edge of its seats; other times, just occasionally, the sparks would backfire and between them they could almost tear a production to pieces.

This evening, quite definitely, the audience was on the edge of its seats. No question but that Saul was dancing flat out, giving full value for money, even over and above – and yet there was something about his performance which Jessamy found worrying. She knew Saul's dancing well enough, and this was not how she had ever seen him dance before. There was a reckless-ness about it which was going to spell disaster if he wasn't very careful. Belinda Tarrant obviously felt it, too, for at the end she said, 'I'm just going back to have a few words with Saul. You and Karen go and wait for me out front.'

Jessamy knew better, for once, than to insist on going backstage with her.

'That was fantastic!' said Karen. 'Didn't you think that was fantastic?'

'Dangerous,' said Jessamy.

'How do you mean, dangerous?'

'Riding for a fall,' said Jessamy. It was one of her dad's expressions. 'He'll injure himself, for sure.'

On Monday, her face bright pink with righteous indignation on Saul's behalf, Karen showed Jessamy an article written by Eric Lauder saying that in City Ballet's new production of *Giselle* Saul Hart had given 'the performance of a lifetime as Albrecht'.

'*He* doesn't say he was riding for a fall.'

No, because he didn't know Saul like Jessamy did. Even the great Eric Lauder couldn't get it right all the time.

'He's dancing again next Saturday... *Swan Lake* with Gemma Dugard. Shall we go?'

'Can if you like,' said Jessamy. 'If he hasn't done himself an injury by then.' Which almost certainly he would have done, dancing like a madman. 'It's very irresponsible,' said Jessamy, 'just because – '

''Cause what?'

Oh, well! She would have to know some time.

''Cause he and Ken have had some stupid quarrel and aren't together any more.'

'Oh, poor Saul!' said Karen. And then, as an afterthought: 'Poor Ken!'

'Mum says he was a stable-izing influence, and now he's not there Saul's gone all to pieces.'

'He's probably unhappy,' said Karen.

'That doesn't mean he has to behave like an idiot! I mean, goodness, Jack and the Bottler used to quarrel all the time. They broke off their engagement twice. Jack didn't go round like some tragedy queen.'

'She's obviously more like you,' said Karen.

Jessamy looked at her, sharply. Had there been a note of criticism in Karen's voice?

'What d'you mean, more like me?'

'More like you than like Saul.'

'What's that supposed to mean?'

'Well – ' Karen hesitated.

'*Well*?' said Jessamy. 'Go on!'

'You're getting really hard,' mumbled Karen.

'*Hard*? Just 'cause I think a professional should behave like a professional?'

'You don't take people's feelings into account.'

'You can't afford to,' said Jessamy, 'not when an audience has paid to see you. You've got to go on and dance for them, it doesn't matter *how* you're feeling. You've still got to do it.'

'Saul did do it!'

'Yes, but he took stupid risks and I bet that's what Mum went round for afterwards, to tell him to pull himself together. I mean, *honestly*,' said Jessamy, 'just 'cause he's had a quarrel with someone – and I bet it was his fault, anyway. I bet he was behaving like a prima donna. Ken wouldn't. Well, would he?'

'I don't know,' muttered Karen. 'I don't know how he'd behave.'

'I thought you said he was so nice? I thought you s –'

'I don't want to discuss it with you,' said Karen. 'Sometimes I don't think you have any feelings at all.'

Now it seemed that Saul wasn't the only one who had quarrelled; Karen and Jessamy had, as well. It was the first time it had ever happened – the first time Karen had ever stuck to her guns and not backed down. *Sometimes I don't think you have any feelings at all.* She did have feelings! She loved Saul more than she loved any other member of her family, but it was silly to risk injuring himself just because he'd fallen out with Ken. People fell out with each other all the time; it was no big deal. And she bet it *was* Saul's fault. Too used to getting his own way, that was his trouble. He had always been Mum's favourite.

For the rest of the week, an uneasy truce existed between Karen and Jessamy. They travelled in to school together in the morning and they travelled back home together in the evening, but instead of sitting next to each other in the school canteen at lunch times they would sit at opposite ends of the table, or wedged in between other people, and instead of chatting to each other as they changed for ballet class Karen would chat to Nella and Maggot while Jessamy – goodness only knew how it happened – found herself increasingly thrown together with Ginny and Lorraine.

On Friday evening the telephone rang, and it was for Jessamy.

'Hallo?' said Jessamy.

'Hi,' said a voice she didn't recognize. 'This is Val – Valentine Harper. We met at Ginny's party.'

'Oh, yes! I remember,' said Jessamy. Divine Val with the blue eyes and the funny little dimple in his chin.

'I was wondering – if you're not doing anything else – whether you'd care to come and see a film with me tomorrow? They're showing something called *The Red Shoes*. It's all about ballet.'

Jessamy beamed into the telephone. She had seen *The Red Shoes* so many times she knew if off by heart.

'I'd love to,' she said.

It was only after they had arranged where to meet and Jessamy had put the telephone down that she remembered: she had agreed to go to the ballet with Karen, to see Saul in *Swan Lake*. Oh, what a drear! Now she would have to ring Karen and tell her she couldn't go, and Karen would think she was getting her own back because of Karen saying she had no feelings, whereas it wasn't that at all, it was just that she had seen *Swan Lake* even more times than she had seen *The Red Shoes*. She had seen Saul dance Siegfried at least half a dozen times, and really one did need to expand one's horizons just occasionally. *The Red Shoes* might be *about* ballet, but it wasn't actually *a* ballet, and it would make a change to talk to someone who had nothing whatsoever to do with the world of dance.

It still wasn't going to be easy, telling Karen.

10

'Surely you can find someone else to go with?' said Jessamy.

At the other end of the telephone, there was silence.

'I mean, Nella or Maggot or . . . someone.'

More silence.

'I mean, *look*,' said Jessamy, 'if you're worried about your gran's telephone bill, *I* could ring them up and ask them. Shall I?'

'I can do it myself,' said Karen.

So what was the problem?

'You could still go back and see Saul. He wouldn't mind. He likes people going to see him.'

That was why Ken had been good for him: he'd stayed at home more, and gone to bed earlier, and not spent half the night at parties, drinking too much. He would burn himself out, said Mum, if he didn't stop burning the candle at both ends.

'If you do go backstage,' said Jessamy (though of course she wouldn't, she would be far too shy) 'tell him that *I* think he ought to make it up with Ken and say he's sorry for whatever it was he did to upset him.'

'How do you know it was Saul?' said Karen, rising up immediately in Saul's defence. Ken might be really, really nice and next door to a saint, but she didn't have a thing about him as she had about Saul.

125

'I know 'cause he's my brother and I know what he's like . . . *spoilt*,' said Jessamy.

'Of course, you're not,' said Karen.

Jessamy held the receiver away from her ear and looked at it.

'No,' she said, 'I'm not.' Nobody was nagged at and ticked off more than Jessamy. Even Karen was having a go at her now. 'Look, I'm really sorry,' she said, 'but I've seen him dance Siegfried so often, and I'm sure Maggot would love to go with you. Or Nella. Or you could even ring Tammy. She lives near. Have you got her number?'

'Probably,' said Karen.

'Well, give her a go. I bet she'd love to see you . . . she could spend the whole time telling you how much better the Royal Ballet does things.'

'Humph!' said Karen.

Jessamy had a bit of a conscience the next day, as she prepared to catch the train into town (she was meeting Val in Piccadilly, 'by the statue of Eros') but only a bit because after all Karen was experienced enough by now to go to the ballet by herself. *And* to go backstage and see Saul, if she could only summon up the courage. In fact it would probably do her good; it wasn't right that she should be dependent on Jessamy all the time. It would be different if it were an evening performance, because of getting home on the tube, late at night. Not even Jessamy would like to do that on her own. But this was a matinée, and it wouldn't even be dark – well, not very dark. Anyway, if Tammy went with her they could travel home together.

The Red Shoes was lovely, and just as Jessamy

126

remembered it from the last time she had seen it (six months ago, on video, with Karen). She still shed a few tears at poor Moira Shearer dancing herself to death. She wished she were old enough to have seen Moira Shearer on stage. Mum was; just. Jessamy sometimes thought that Moira Shearer looked rather like Mum, with her beautiful red hair and pale skin.

Afterwards, Val took her to a pizza place and bought her a pizza, checking first that she was allowed to eat them.

'There are an awful lot of things that dancers aren't allowed to eat, aren't there?'

'Yes, there are.' Jessamy said it with feeling: she had just seen a large plateful of chips being delivered to the next table.

'Ginny's always grumbling about it . . . she only has to eat one square of chocolate and she puts on weight.'

'Does she?' It was cheering to know that even the great Ginny Alexander had problems. Sometimes, just recently, Jessamy had begun to think she might be the only one.

'How did you like the film?' said Val.

'Oh, I loved it! I always do. It doesn't matter how many times you see it, I – I mean – ' Jessamy floundered.

'You mean,' said Val with a grin, 'you've seen it before.'

'Well – yes. But not for ages. I'd practically forgotten what happened.'

'Liar! I bet you know it off by heart. I'd never heard of it,' said Val, 'but when I told Ginny where we were going she said, "She'll have seen it at least a dozen times." Very *crushingly*.'

'Well, it doesn't matter,' said Jessamy, 'it was nice of you to think of it.' Most boys wouldn't have done. Most boys would have wanted to take her to something bloody and violent. Politely, she added, 'I hope you weren't too bored by it.'

'Bored?' Val sounded surprised. 'Why should I be bored?'

'Boys usually are.' It was Jessamy's experience that boys as a whole considered ballet a poofy thing to do. You had to be pretty brave, if you were a boy, to put up with all the jeers and sneers of your mates.

'I wasn't bored,' said Val. 'I do a bit of dancing myself.'

'Really?' said Jessamy.

'Ice dancing. Have you ever done that?'

Slowly, Jessamy shook her head.

'Would you like to try it some time? I should think you'd be quite good at it. You could come down the rink with me next Saturday. It'd be a bit crowded, but at least you could get the feel of it.'

Jessamy wrestled silently with her conscience. She probably would be good at ice dancing – but would ice dancing be good for her? She had been trying really hard this term, working on her attitude problem, being humble, being less bouncy. The lists would be going up soon for the end-of-term show. Every year in July there was a special choreographers' evening, when the juniors danced in short pieces choreographed by some of the senior students. This year the theme was fairy tales. The possibilities were endless . . . Snow White, Cinder-

128

ella, Sleeping Beauty . . . Jessamy was determined to get a part in one of them. And by part she meant *part*, not just another mouldy peasant pas de deux.

'Is ice skating one of the things you're not allowed to do?' said Val.

Jessamy sighed. She knew what Mum would say: 'For heaven's sake, Jessamy! You either want to be a dancer or you don't.'

'I thought it might be,' said Val. There was regret in his voice. Now, thought Jessamy, he won't want to see me again. 'You do have to lead a terribly restricted life, don't you? Still, I suppose it's worth it in the long run – unless you end up in the corps. I should think that must be a grind.'

'I'm never going to be in the corps,' said Jessamy.

'Never? But don't you have to start off that way?'

'Oh, well, yes; just at the beginning. But if I thought I was going to be stuck there, I'd –

'What?'

'I'd go ice skating!' said Jessamy.

On Sunday morning, being still just a little bit bothered by conscience, she rang Karen.

'How was *Swan Lake*? Did you go?'

'Yes, we all went,' said Karen.

'*All*? Who's all?'

'Me and Nella, and Maggot and Tammy.'

'All four of you?'

'Yes,' said Karen. 'It was fun.'

Well, that was all right; Jessamy had had fun, too. (After eating their pizzas she and Val had walked along Shaftesbury Avenue looking at the theatres, and then down Charing Cross Road to look at the book shops and the ballet shops, and then to the Embankment, to catch the train home.)

'So what was *Swan Lake* like?'

'It was good,' said Karen.

'What about my soppy brother?'

There was a pause; then in a small voice Karen said: 'Saul didn't dance.'

Oh, *didn't* he? Surprise, surprise!

'What's he done?' said Jessamy. 'Broken his neck?'

'I don't know. They just made an announcement that Mark Allmond was taking his place.'

That wouldn't have pleased people; but I won't say I told you so, thought Jessamy. I am bigger than that.

'Don't worry,' she said, 'it can't be anything serious or I'd have heard. Mum would be bound to know. Shall I ring him up and ask him?'

'Oh, no, Jessamy, don't!' said Karen.

'Why not? I think I will. I want to know what he's done.'

'Couldn't you ask your mum?' said Karen.

'Mum's not here. I'm going to ring Saul. I'll call you back and report.'

'Don't be unkind to him,' begged Karen.

Why not? thought Jessamy. She wouldn't be, of course, but she didn't see why she shouldn't just ring and ask him. After all, he was her brother.

'Not you again!' groaned Saul, when Jessamy brightly said 'Hallo!' into the receiver.

'You told me I could ring you.'

'All right, Nosey! So what do you want to know?

You want to know why I wasn't on last night? My God, the bush telegraph works quickly, doesn't it?'

Jessamy, not knowing what a bush telegraph was, said: 'Karen went specially to see you.'

'So tell Karen I am exceedingly sorry but I have torn a muscle in my calf. There! Does that satisfy you?'

'I knew you'd go and do something like that,' said Jessamy. 'That night when we came to see you – '

'Please! Spare me the lecture!'

'Are you and Ken an item again yet?'

'Go stuff yourself in a bottle!' said Saul; but he didn't say it as if he were mad at her, so maybe, thought Jessamy, he was getting over it. Or maybe he and Ken had made it up.

'You ought to try asking Ken,' said Jessamy, when she rang Karen back. 'Next time you go and sit for him.'

'I couldn't ask him a thing like that!' said Karen, horrified. 'And anyway, he doesn't need me to sit for him any more. He's made all the sketches he wants, he just has to put in the finishing touches.'

'And then what?' said Jessamy. 'The National Portrait Gallery?'

Karen, very seriously, said, 'Don't they only have famous people there?'

'Oh, well, one day,' said Jessamy, 'when you're an international star . . .'

On Monday the lists went up for the choreographers' evening. The second years were to dance Cinderella, Snow White, and Sleeping Beauty.

131

The cast list for Cinderella was:

Cinders	*Nella Stevens*
Prince Charming	*John McDonald*
Ugly Sisters	*Nicky Scott, Jason Berry*
Buttons	*Margaret Moorhouse*
Fairy Godmother	*Lorraine Hooper*

The cast list for Snow White was:

Snow White	*Karen Anders*
Wicked Witch	*Simon Banks*

And the cast list for Sleeping Beauty:

Princess Aurora	*Carolyn Britten* (an incredibly thin girl with enviable bone structure and enormous blue eyes)
Prince	*Daniel Porter*

Jessamy was one of the Seven Dwarves; it was almost worse than being part of a peasant pas de deux.

The only (very slight) consolation was that Ginny was also a Dwarf. It was a puzzle to everyone why neither she nor Jessamy had been given proper parts when all were agreed they were two of the strongest dancers.

'There's got to be *some* reason,' said Karen.

'I think I know why Ginny was left out.' It was Maggot who volunteered the information. 'I was in the office talking to Miss Treacher about something and

132

Madam came in and put some papers down just near me and I couldn't help seeing,' said Maggot. 'I mean they were *upside down* but I can read things upside down quite easily, and I could see they were reports on people and the first one was Ginny and I just had time to read "Technique strong but query content. Keep on hold?" And then Madam put a folder on top and I couldn't see any more.'

'What does it mean,' pondered Nella, 'technique strong but query content?'

'It means it's all show,' said Maggot.

'No soul,' said Karen.

They decided, as they thought about Ginny's dancing, that maybe it was true. She was brilliant, but perhaps just a bit flashy.

'But you can't say that about Jessamy!' cried Karen.

The others agreed that you certainly couldn't.

'Jessamy is *dramatic*,' said Nella.

Jessamy tried her best to make light of it – 'Maybe Madam doesn't like dramatic dancers!' – but inside herself she felt the thick oily gunge of hurt and resentment begin to churn and bubble. After all her hard work – all her striving to be humble and have the right attitude. What was the point of trying if you were just going to be overlooked all the time?

'Makes you sick!' fumed Ginny, finding herself alone in the changing room one day with Jessamy. 'For two pins I'd leave this lousy rotten dump and go elsewhere.'

Jessamy knew how she felt.

On Thursday, Valentine rang up. He wanted to know

whether he was going to be seeing Jessamy again this Saturday, and if so what she would like to do?

'We could go and see a ballet if you wanted.'

'I'm sick of seeing ballet! It's all I ever get to see.'

She didn't mean to be ungracious, but just at the moment she was sick of ballet full stop. For two pins she would ask Mum if she could leave CBS and go somewhere that did drama, instead. Or at least drama as *well*. Arts Educational, for instance, or Elmhurst. They might appreciate her there. (*She has an instinctive feel for words and drama . . .*)

'Why don't you take me ice skating?' said Jessamy.

'Skating?' He sounded startled. 'I thought you weren't meant to do that?'

'I can do whatever I want,' said Jessamy.

Val had predicted that she would be good at skating, and she was. Her ballet training came in useful. She had no trouble at all in balancing, not even in the first dangerous moment of stepping on to the ice, which Val had warned her about. (He had also warned her to dust her feet with antiseptic powder before leaving home – 'You'll have to hire some boots at the rink. You don't want to run the risk of catching athlete's foot.' He was very solicitous of her.)

By the end of the first session Jessamy had learnt how to start, how to stop, how to skate in a curve, and how to do what Val called 'a cross-over', crossing her right foot in front of her left at the end of a curve, which sounded complicated but in fact, for a dancer, was really quite simple. He also taught her how to skate backwards, which rather curiously turned out to be even easier than skating forwards, except that you had

134

to start from a position of bent knees and toes turned in, which to Jessamy, accustomed to the turned-out position of classical ballet, seemed ugly and unnatural.

'No, it looks fine!' Val assured her. 'Next time I'll t –' He stopped.

'Next time I want to do something difficult,' said Jessamy. 'I want to do one of those jumps they do.'

'I don't know about jumps,' said Val.

'I want to!' said Jessamy; and she did.

Over the next few weeks she mastered runs, backward cross-overs, crossed chassés, circle eights – four different types – changes of edge, a variety of turns, including one called 'inside Mohawk', and even a simple dance. Val said he had never known anyone learn so fast.

'We might even be able to go in for competitions together!'

Jessamy wasn't so sure about that. Going in for competitions meant getting up early in the morning to use the rink when it wasn't crowded, and that was something she didn't think she would be able to keep from her mum. Marisol would notice, and would ask questions, and then Jessamy would have to make up some story, and she was bound to be found out; she always was. So far, all Belinda Tarrant knew was that Jessamy had a boyfriend (the entire family, including Saul, seemed to think this was hilarious). She had no idea what Jessamy was actually getting up to. Val, on the other hand, had no idea that her mum didn't know. Karen knew because Jessamy had told her. Defiantly she had said, 'I can't come to the ballet with you because I'm going ice skating with Val.'

'Ice skating?' Karen's eyes, predictably, had grown round as saucepan lids. 'Jessamy, that's dangerous! You could injure yourself.'

'So what?' said Jessamy. Saul had injured himself, and no one had bawled *him* out. She bet when Belinda Tarrant had gone backstage to talk to him it had been all lovey dovey and 'Darling, I know you're unhappy but you really must take care.' Well, Jessamy was unhappy, too! Clumping about being a Dwarf while other people got to dance proper roles.

Timidly – Jessamy had not been in the best of tempers just lately – Karen said, 'What about your public?'

'What *public*?'

'All the people that are coming to the end-of-term show.' Jessamy was the one who had said that a dancer ought not to let her personal life interfere with her professional one. 'If you got injured, you wouldn't be able to dance.'

Jessamy tossed her head. 'They could find someone else!'

'But that wouldn't be fair,' said Karen. 'It wouldn't be fair to the people that are coming to see you.'

'Nobody's coming to see me!' Who wanted to come and see a dwarf? She hadn't even told her mum and dad yet.

Stubbornly, Karen said, 'It still wouldn't be fair to the rest of the cast.'

'Pooh! It wouldn't make an atom of difference,' said Jessamy.

'Yes, it would! Someone else would have to learn the part at the last moment –'

'Lucky them!'

' – and it would affect the whole performance. And anyway,' urged Karen, 'think of the damage you could do! You could injure yourself permanently.'

'Oh, stop being so nunlike! I'm only going ice skating, not climbing Mount Everest.'

That Saturday at the rink Val said earnestly, 'Jessamy, you know what you said a few weeks ago, about being sick of ballet?'

'Mm,' said Jessamy.

'Are you still sick of it?'

'Yes, I am!' said Jessamy. 'I'm sick to death of it!'

''Cause I was thinking,' said Val, 'why don't you ask your mother if you could take up ice dancing seriously?'

'Seriously?' Jessamy was startled.

'Yes! And then we could practise together and be a pair and go in for competitions . . . we might even,' said Val, 'reach Olympic standard!'

'She wouldn't let me,' said Jessamy.

'Not even if you came along to meet my coach and he had a word with her?'

'She still wouldn't let me,' said Jessamy. 'She doesn't really believe that ice dancing is a – a proper art form. Not compared to ballet. She's very snobbish that way. It's 'cause of ballet dancers needing all those years of training and ballet going back to people like Pavlova, and Diaghilev and Fokine and – and Nijinsky and that. Ice dancing's more a sort of – a sort of sport, really,' said Jessamy, 'isn't it? I mean, I know you have to practise tremendously hard and get up early in the morning, but it's not the same as working at the barre

137

every day and knowing that you're doing just what Pavlova used to do, and Fonteyn and Ulanova and Markova, and – .' Her voice trailed away.

'That was you talking,' said Val, 'wasn't it? Not just your mother.' He didn't sound accusing; only a bit hurt. '*You* don't think it's a proper art form.'

'I do!' said Jessamy; but her face fired up and gave her away. 'I do, honestly, but – ' She couldn't imagine devoting her life to it.

'You're only doing it to be defiant, aren't you?' said Val. 'Does your mother even know about it?'

'No!' Jessamy sprang to her feet.

'In that case, you shouldn't be doing it. Jessamy!' Val made a lunge as Jessamy leapt forward on to the ice. They had just announced a speed session, which Val never let her join in. He always said that speed merchants were only out for a good time and didn't care about the quality of their skating.

'Jessamy, you idiot! Come back!'

Jessamy laughed and dashed off across the ice. She was going to be a speed merchant and have a good time!

It was exhilarating, flying round the ice rink (everyone going anti-clockwise, to avoid accidents). It would have been even more exhilarating if someone in front of her – some dumb clod who should never have been allowed there in the first place – hadn't tripped over his own stupid feet and gone sprawling. Jessamy was moving too fast to avoid him. Head over heels went Jessamy; crash bang wallop on to the ice. Even then she would have picked herself up and happily continued, had it not been for Val, sprinting along behind her and catching at her arm.

'Jessamy, for – '

'Ow!' screamed Jessamy. For a dreadful moment, she thought she might be going to faint.

Val's forehead crinkled into a frown of concern. 'Don't say you've gone and broken something . . . that'll put the cat amongst the pigeons!'

She hadn't broken anything – she was tougher than that – but her wrist swelled up like a waterlogged balloon and had to be put into a crepe bandage and kept in a sling 'for at least forty-eight hours'.

'How did you *do* it?' wailed her mum.

'Tripped over,' said Jessamy.

'It's those ridiculous shoes you insist on wearing!'

The ridiculous shoes were her trainers – extremely expensive trainers. Jessamy didn't bother explaining to her mum that trainers were the last sort of shoes to cause you to trip. If Belinda Tarrant thought her shoes were responsible, so much the better.

'What happened?' said Karen, on Monday morning; but she could guess. She didn't say 'I told you so' because Jessamy hadn't said it when Saul had had to be replaced in *Swan Lake* and it wouldn't have been fair, but she did hope that now Jessamy would come to her senses and not just toss her head and carry on.

You could never be quite sure, with Jessamy; she was someone who hated to be proved wrong. And of course she was only doing it because of not being given a proper part in the choreographic evening. Karen couldn't understand why they kept passing her over.

Jessamy was a good dancer – one of the best in the class. What were they trying to do? Break her spirit?

There was much talk that day about one of their year, Carolyn Britten, the thin girl with the big blue eyes, having been diagnosed as anorexic and suspended until she had got back up to her proper weight.

'She'll never manage to do it by the end of term,' said Ginny – gloatingly, or so it seemed to Jessamy.

'She might not do it at all,' said Maggot. 'I knew a dancer that was anorexic and she just faded away to nothing.'

Ginny didn't seem interested in dancers fading away to nothing: she seemed interested only in Carolyn's 'not managing to do it' by the end of term. Of course! The penny dropped. Carolyn had been dancing Princess Aurora. It'll be between Ginny and me, thought Jessamy; and her heart beat faster and her palms started sweating in spite of herself. She still hadn't told Mum about being cast as a Dwarf. If she could only go home and say that she was dancing Sleeping Beauty!

Later that day she was kept behind by Miss Eldon.

'Jessamy, this wrist of yours ... how long is it going to keep you out of commission?'

Jessamy's heart thudded and roared. 'Only ab-bout a w-week, the doctor says.'

'Good! Because Marguerite, who choreographed Sleeping Beauty, would like you to take over Carolyn's role. I told her I was sure you could manage to learn it in time, you're a very quick study. I take it that will present you with no problems?'

The biggest beam ever spread across Jessamy's face.

It was so big that she couldn't speak through it. Vigorously, she shook her head. Miss Eldon smiled.

'Well, it looks as if this is your chance . . . make the most of it!'

'I will!' promised Jessamy.

11

'You're dancing Princess Aurora? Oh, Jessamy, that is good news! Let me give you a kiss.' Belinda Tarrant hugged Jessamy to her in one of her rare embraces. 'Your father will be so happy! Mind you, they've left the casting rather late, haven't they?'

'Oh! Well.' Jessamy shrugged. 'There was a bit of a mix-up.'

'What about Karen? What is she dancing?'

'She's dancing Snow White.'

'Very appropriate. Good! Both my star pupils distinguishing themselves. I take it we are allowed to come and watch?'

'You *want* to come and watch?' said Jessamy.

'Well, of course I do! Your first leading role – '

'There won't be any proper pas de deux work. We don't start that till we're in our third year.'

'Yes, I do remember!' Belinda Tarrant laughed. 'It's not that long since Saul was there ... sometimes it doesn't seem that long since I was, though goodness knows it's getting on for forty years.' She gave Jessamy another hug. 'I'm really very pleased for you, darling, and for Karen, too. It's been a long time coming, but I knew you'd get there!'

Saul rang later that evening, specially to talk to Jessamy. She thought that perhaps Mum had told him about her dancing Princess Aurora, and that he was ringing to congratulate her, but it wasn't that at all.

'Now who's done something stupid and injured herself?' jeered Saul.

'How did you get to hear about it?'

'I told you, the bush telegraph works fast . . . clear your throat and sooner or later the whole world knows.'

'Well, mine is only a *little* injury,' said Jessamy. 'Not enough to stop me dancing . . . I'm going to dance Princess Aurora in Sleeping Beauty at the end of term.'

'What a grotesque piece of miscasting! Are they going to give you a mask?'

'Don't be horrible,' said Jessamy. Ken might not have wanted to paint her, but she wasn't as bad as all that. In fact everyone said she looked like Saul, and Saul was really quite handsome. Sometimes. When he bothered to shave and comb his hair and didn't drink too much and go to bed late. 'Are you being sensible now?' she said.

'Come again?'

'Have you *stable*-ized yourself?'

'Oh, absolutely! Steady as a rock. After all, I have to set an example to my little sister, don't I? Can't have her going off the rails!'

For the first time in a long time, Jessamy felt that she was not only *on* the rails but knew where they were leading. All the doubts and uncertainties of the past few months had disappeared. Once again, she had a goal in life: she was going to be a dancer!

Next morning, on the way in to school, she told Karen what Belinda Tarrant had said.

'She's really pleased. She and Dad are both going to come and watch. Is your gran?'

'Yes! She says she wouldn't miss it for worlds,' said Karen.

'Does she feel all right, now, about you being at ballet school?'

'I think she's got used to it. She just worries sometimes that I don't eat enough.'

'Oh, but you eat like a horse!' Karen was one of the lucky few who could stuff herself as much as she liked and not put on an ounce. 'Nobody's ever going to tell *you* you've got a big tail,' said Jessamy.

'Well, you haven't, either! Not compared to normal people.'

Maybe not, but that was the trouble, wasn't it? Dancers *couldn't* be compared to normal people.

Jessamy shot a furtive sideways glance at herself in a shop window.

'I'm going to go on a diet,' she said. 'I'm going to lose at least half a stone by the end of term!'

Karen looked at her, doubtfully. 'You know what Miss Eldon says about people going on diets . . . they end up like Carolyn.'

'Not always; not if they're sensible. And anyway –' Jessamy slapped a disdainful hand against her backside – 'you can't have Aurora with a big tail!'

As they went up to the canteen at lunch time they bumped into Marguerite Dalloway, the senior who had choreographed Sleeping Beauty.

'Jessamy Hart!' She beckoned to Jessamy, furiously. 'You *are* a selfish little idiot, aren't you?'

Jessamy blinked. What had she done now?

144

'Just as we'd got everything settled!'

'I don't know what you're t-talking about,' stammered Jessamy.

'You'll find out soon enough! Madam wants to see you in her office immediately after lunch.'

Marguerite went stalking off, her back stiff with outrage.

'What did she want?' said Karen, as Jessamy rejoined her at the top of the stairs.

'Oh, nothing! I don't know.' Jessamy said it uneasily. It quite plainly wasn't nothing; not if Madam wanted to see her.

She tried hard to pretend, as she trailed along the corridors to Madam's office (after her new diet lunch of salad and yoghurt) that Madam was going to announce something stupendous and wonderful, such as that Jessamy, alone of all her year, had been chosen to take part in one of the Company productions and as a result wouldn't be able to dance in the end-of-term show. That would account for Marguerite being so mad at her.

It was a beautiful idea, but she knew in her heart that it was only make-believe. She couldn't help remembering, now that she looked back on it, the dark frown that had rippled across Miss Eldon's brow in morning class as she had contemplated Jessamy with her strapped-up wrist. She had wondered at the time what she could have done to incur Miss Eldon's wrath.

With chin held high, she knocked at Madam's door. What was it her dad had always said to her, as a small child, on her way to the dentist? 'The coward dies a thousand deaths, the hero dies but one.' Jessamy would

145

face the worst when it happened – *if* it happened. But who knew? Perhaps it never would.

She heard Madam's voice, light and sharp, call, 'Come!' Jessamy opened the door and walked through – and knew immediately that the worst had arrived. Her beautiful idea had indeed been make-believe. Whatever Madam was going to tell her, it was not that she had been singled out to dance in a Company production.

'Well, Jessamy.' Madam sat, small and imperious, behind her outsize desk. Madam's desk wasn't cluttered as most people's were. It had two telephones, two wire baskets containing letters, a blotter, and a desk-tidy with little scooped-out sections for pens and pencils, and paper clips and rubbers. Everything was in its allotted place, very neat and precise, just like Madam.

'Sit down, please.' Madam indicated a high-backed chair on the opposite side of the desk. Jessamy sat down nervously on the extreme edge of it.

'I had hoped, Jessamy, that this term would see an improvement in your attitude.' Madam's lips compressed themselves into a thin, grim line of displeasure. 'This has evidently not happened. I understand you have been ice skating and that is how you injured your wrist.'

Jessamy's cheeks fired up. Who had told Madam that she had been ice skating? Nobody knew! (A small voice inside her said, Karen knew . . . She pushed the thought to the back of her mind.)

'I take it this is true?' said Madam.

Jessamy struggled for a moment.

'I think you have answered the question. You will

146

not be dancing in the end-of-term show; I shall tell Marguerite to find someone else. It is hard on her, for in fact you were her first choice. I was the one who stepped in originally and vetoed the suggestion. You may find it instructive to know why. Quite simply, I did not consider you ready to be entrusted with a leading role. Oh, I have no doubts as to your technical ability! None whatsoever. But frankly you have yet to convince me of your ... integrity. Your commitment to the dance. I wonder, Jessamy – '

Madam sat back in her chair, her hands resting on the arms.

'I wonder if you have ever asked yourself why it was that we hesitated to take you in the first place? Possibly you never realized that we hesitated. But we did! You were one of our borderline cases. Had it not been for another student opting at the last moment to go elsewhere – ' Madam's lip curled slightly as she said it: Madam had scant regard for elsewhere – 'the probability is that you would not have been offered a place. It seemed to me then, as it seems to me now, that your attitude towards your studies is somewhat ... how shall I put it? Cavalier?'

Jessamy sat in silence. She couldn't have spoken even if Madam had expected her to, which quite obviously she didn't.

'We ask a great deal of our students. We ask for total dedication. Nothing less, Jessamy, will satisfy us. We can always tell, you know, what a student is thinking. We can spot the one who values outside interests more than the ballet. We can spot the one who starts to wonder whether it's all really worth it – the one who feels rebellious – the one who gives up caring. It all comes out in their work. Technique can cover a multitude of sins; but what it cannot do is disguise the basic attitude. I was very much hoping – '

Madam leaned forward again, making a steeple of her hands.

' – very much hoping that your attitude had changed for the better. Miss Eldon gave me encouraging reports. That is why, when Marguerite needed a replacement in her ballet, I allowed her to revert to her first choice. I have rarely been so deceived or felt so disappointed!'

Jessamy opened her mouth – then shut it again. But too late. Madam's eyes were sharp: they missed nothing.

'You wished to say something? Something by way of excuse, perhaps?'

Jessamy pursed her lips.

'Please say it,' said Madam.

When Madam said please, it was an order rather than a request.

'I can still dance,' mumbled Jessamy. 'I've only – ' she waved her wrist, feebly – 'only sprained it.'

She knew at once – had known even before she said it – that it was the wrong thing. The storm clouds gathered on Madam's brow. Her eyes shot splinters of ice across the desk.

'That is exactly the sort of attitude of which I am complaining! Do you suppose it makes one iota of difference *what* you have done to it? For you to go ice skating at all, whether or not you sustain an injury, is sufficient to betray your lack of commitment. Such a student can have no place in this school. I am seriously considering, Jessamy, whether to ask your parents to withdraw you. I believe we made a grave mistake in allowing you to come here.'

The worst had happened – and never in her life had Jessamy found anything so hard to face up to. There had been times before, times when she had been in trouble, when fate had caught up with her; always she had shrugged them off. If she felt that she had deserved it she had been honest enough to say so and accept her punishment. If she felt she had been hard done by she had poured out her troubles to Saul or defiantly sworn that 'she didn't care!' But this time she did care – and this time there was nothing to be gained from pouring out her troubles, to Saul or to anyone else. If Madam had made up her mind, then nobody, not even Saul, for all he was one of her favourites, probably not even Mum or Dad, would talk her into changing it.

And would Mum and Dad want to? Mum would say, 'You've let us down, Jessamy!' And Jessamy would know that it was true. She *shouldn't* have gone ice skating. But it was Madam's fault for not letting Marguerite cast her as Princess Aurora in the first place! If Madam hadn't gone and interfered, none of this would ever have happened. Her attitude *had* changed. But how could you help feeling hurt and angry when you kept being overlooked all the time and no one seemed to have any faith in you? Oh, it wasn't fair! It wasn't fair!

Jessamy felt a strong temptation simply to grab her bag and her coat and run away. If there was one thing that stopped her it wasn't pride – her pride had taken too great a battering – it was the small, almost infinitesimal, ray of hope contained in the words 'seriously considering'. Surely that meant Madam hadn't *quite* made up her mind? So that if Jessamy behaved as good as gold for the rest of the term . . .

Slim though the chance was, it was the only one she had.

'Did I see you coming out of Madam's office earlier on?' said Lorraine, during the afternoon break.

'No,' said Jessamy. She said it boldly, looking Lorraine directly in the eye as she spoke.

'That's funny,' said Lorraine.

'Yes, isn't it?' said Jessamy. 'Ha ha!'

It wasn't any of their business, what Madam had said.

When it came to going-home time, Jessamy was first into the cloakroom and first out of it, running as fast as she could through the streets to Waterloo. She didn't think she could bear to travel home with Karen. Karen had betrayed her. Her best friend, whom she had helped to get to ballet school, and she had betrayed her! Tears stung the backs of Jessamy's eyes as she paced the platform, waiting for the tube. Why had Karen done it? She couldn't be jealous, for she had nothing, any more, to be jealous of. Was it because of Jessamy not going to see *Swan Lake* with her? But that had been weeks ago! She couldn't still be cross. And even if she were –

The tube came in and Jessamy jumped on to it, praying for the doors to close before anyone from ballet school appeared. Even if Karen *were* still cross with her, to go and tell Madam, or Miss Eldon, or whoever it was she had told, that Jessamy had sprained her wrist going ice skating, was the lowest, meanest thing that anyone could do. I shall never forgive her, thought Jessamy. Never!

Marisol was in the hall, speaking on the telephone, when Jessamy burst through the front door.

'Why, Yessamy – ' she broke off in concern, placing one hand across the mouthpiece as Jessamy slammed the front door behind her and headed for the stairs. 'Qué te pasa?'

'Nothing!'

In the privacy of her bedroom, Jessamy threw herself on the bed and wept. Marisol came after her, tapping at the door calling, 'Yessamy! Yessamy! Please tell me what is wrong!' but Jessamy only yelled at her to 'Go away and leave me alone!'

Minutes later, someone else tapped at the door. Saul's voice said, 'Jess? Are you going to let me in?'

Jessamy sat up and scrubbed at her eyes. 'Door's not locked.'

'I know, but – ' Saul came into the room ' – it seemed only polite to ask for permission.'

Jessamy blotted her nose with the pillow. 'What – ' she hiccuped – 'are you doing here?'

'We just popped over to drop off Mum and Dad's present.'

'What p-present?'

'Anniversary present, dumbo. They've been married thirty-five years. Had you forgotten?'

Jessamy sniffed, dolefully. 'It's not till S-Saturday.'

'I know, but we couldn't make it Saturday. I'm on that night.'

Jessamy knew that she ought at least to pretend an

interest, ought at least to ask him what he was dancing, but the tears had welled up again and she couldn't speak for crying.

'Hey, now, kiddo! Come on!' Saul sat down on the bed beside her. He slid an arm round her shoulders. 'It can't be as bad as all that! What's the problem? Someone been beating up on you? Tell me who it is and I'll go and work 'em over!'

He made his hands into fists, trying to jolly her out of it. Jessamy attempted a watery smile, but it didn't work. The corners of her mouth refused to move in any direction save down.

'So it is as bad as all that, eh?'

Miserably, she nodded.

'Want to tell me about it?'

Slowly, between sniffs and hiccups, Jessamy sobbed out her story – how Marguerite had chosen her to dance Princess Aurora but Madam had said no and so Jessamy had gone ice skating and had sprained her wrist only no one need ever have known if Karen hadn't gone and split on her and now she wasn't going to be allowed to dance Aurora even though Marguerite still wanted her and Madam was even hinting – gasp, hiccup – that she might ask M-Mum and D-Dad to withd-draw me from the sc-chool!

Saul listened in grave silence.

'It seems to me,' he said at last, 'that you've certainly had a few problems, though from the sound of things you were well on the way to solving them.'

'I was!' wept Jessamy. 'But then Madam went and r-ruined it all!'

'She does seem to have stepped in at just the wrong

psychological moment. But she's not infallible, you know. She likes to think she is, but she can make mistakes the same as anyone else.

'She thinks she made a m-mistake by accepting m-me in the first p-place!'

'Well, that's wrong for a start! From all accounts you'd already begun to get your act together. If she couldn't see that, then that's her shortcoming. I presume,' said Saul, 'that you wouldn't have been stupid enough to go ice skating if you'd been given a decent part?'

'N-no, but – ' Jessamy scrubbed fiercely at her eyes – 'she'd say that j-just went to p-prove that my attitude was still wrong!'

'Yes; and I can see that she might have a point. But you can push people too far. You'd learnt your lesson; she didn't need to rub your nose in it. The thing you have to understand about Madam is that if she can break a person, she will. There are those who are pliant, like Karen; she can bend her whichever way she wants. Then there are others, like you, who fight her every inch of the way. She doesn't care for that. But if you can come through it – '

'L-like you did.'

'It was easier for me. She treats men differently. But Colleen, now – '

Colleen McBride? 'Did she fight her?'

'And how! They hated each other's guts. Still do. But at least they've learnt to respect each other.'

'I respect M-Madam!' Jessamy's tears burst out afresh. 'But she doesn't r-respect m-me!'

'Well, of course she doesn't! She's not going to respect a mere slip of a gel.'

'No, she's going to ask M-Mum and D-Dad to r-remove me!'

'Here, have a hanky,' said Saul. He waited while she blew her nose. 'Would you like me to speak to Mum and Dad for you? Tell them what's happened? The chances are, if they went along and had a word with her – '

'I don't want them doing that! If she doesn't think I'm good enough she can throw me out. I'm not having anyone b-beg for me!'

Saul twitched an eyebrow.

'Pride, pride,' he murmured. 'Don't cut off your nose to spite your face.'

'Well, but it wouldn't do any g-good, anyway,' said Jessamy. '*Would* it? Honestly? If she's made up her mind.'

He bowed his head. 'Possibly not. But I'll still speak to the folks for you if you'd like.'

'It's all right.' Jessamy folded his handkerchief and handed it back to him. 'I'll do it. But I'm not doing it tonight!' She snatched the handkerchief back again. 'I'll do it tomorrow when I'm f-feeling s-stronger.'

'OK. I'll give you a call, see how you've got on. In the meantime – ' Saul held out a hand – 'come down and say hallo to Ken. We'll have a quick coffee before we go off.'

'Coffee's bad for you,' muttered Jessamy. And then, as she followed Saul out of the door: 'Are you an item again?'

'What's that supposed to mean?' said Saul.

'Did you apologize for whatever it was that you did?'

'Me?' said Saul. 'Why me?'

'It's bound to have been you,' said Jessamy. 'You're spoiled!'

Ken was waiting for them down in the basement. Marisol, thankfully, was upstairs having a bath. Jessamy didn't think she could have faced her, all red-eyed and snuffly as she was. She didn't mind so much with Ken.

'I know she's not looking her best,' said Saul, 'but shall we break the news to her?'

'What news?' said Jessamy.

'Ken wants to do a painting of you. God knows why. He wants to put it with the one he did of Karen and call them – pardon me while I politely heave – *The Little Dancers*.'

'If that's all right with you,' said Ken.

This time yesterday she would have been in heaven. Today all she could think was: Karen betrayed me. Who wanted to be painted with someone who had betrayed them?

'I could call it the *young* dancers, if you'd rather.'

'Don't expect I'll be one very much longer,' mumbled Jessamy.

'You will,' said Saul. He felt for her hand under the table and squeezed it. 'One way or another, you'll always be one. I promise!'

12

It wasn't possible to avoid Karen next day, for she was waiting as usual at the entrance to the tube.

'What happened to you last night? Nobody saw you go!'

'I wanted to get home.'

Jessamy pushed rudely past Karen and headed for the ticket barrier. Karen, confused and plainly hurt, hurried after her.

'Jessamy!'

Jessamy swung round. '*What*?'

'Is something wrong?' said Karen.

'What's wrong,' snarled Jessamy, 'is people that are supposed to be a person's best friend going and betraying them!'

Karen's face grew pink and puckered. 'What are you talking about?'

'Why did you tell Madam I'd been ice skating?'

'I didn't!'

'Well, Miss Eldon, then.'

'Jessamy, I didn't! I wouldn't! Why should I do a thing like that?'

Jessamy regarded her through narrowed eyes. 'So, if you didn't, who did?'

'I don't know, but it wasn't me!'

'You must have told *someone*,' said Jessamy.

'I didn't! Truly!'

'Not even Maggot or Nella?'

'No!'

Jessamy walked on, frowning, along the platform. She wanted to believe Karen – but who else could it have been?

'Why, anyway?' Karen asked the question, anxiously. 'Is Madam cross with you?'

Staring fixedly straight ahead, Jessamy said: 'She's taken the part off me and she's threatening to throw me out.'

'Oh, Jessamy! No!'

'Well, she is,' said Jessamy. 'And if you dare to tell anyone – '

'I won't,' said Karen. 'I promise! But, J – '

'I don't want to talk about it.'

Jessamy turned away, before the hot tears of shame and self-pity could engulf her. She had cried all over Saul: she didn't want to cry over Karen. Saul was her brother, and was older than she was. Karen was the same age, and if it hadn't been for Jessamy – a tear plopped off the end of her nose and furiously she dashed at it with the back of her hand – if it hadn't been for Jessamy, Karen would still be struggling on her own, trying to teach herself ballet in her bedroom.

They spent the rest of the journey in silence, Jessamy pretending to go over her maths homework, Karen looking at a ballet magazine. As they left Waterloo and turned off down Lower Marsh there was a shout of, 'Jessamy!' They stopped, and turned. Ginny was chasing after them.

'Jessamy! I hear Marguerite had a go at you. I'm

ever so sorry! I never meant to tell on you, it just slipped out.'

Ginny. Of course! She was Val's cousin, wasn't she? Val would have told her he was taking Jessamy ice skating; he wouldn't have seen any reason not to. And Jessamy had been so sure that it was Karen!

'I do hope,' said Ginny, oozing mock solicitude, 'that they haven't taken the part off you?'

'Why should they take if off her?' said Karen. 'If Jessamy's the one they chose, why should they go and un-choose her?'

'Well, *I* don't think they should, but you know what Madam's like . . . we're supposed to live like *nuns*,' said Ginny.

'Why not go and look at the notice board?' suggested Jessamy. 'If you're that interested.'

'Oh! I'm not interested for myself,' said Ginny. 'I was just worried for you.'

'She did it on purpose,' whispered Karen, as Ginny peeled off to join Angie and Lorraine. 'She went and told on you so she could get your part.'

'And I thought it was you,' said Jessamy. 'I thought you were mad at me for not going to the ballet with you that time.'

'Well, I was,' admitted Karen, 'but I wouldn't ever do a thing like that!'

'I'm sorry.' Jessamy said it humbly. 'I really am. Oh, but how am I going to tell Mum and Dad?'

'Maybe it won't happen,' said Karen.

'It will! Madam's as good as said so. I know I deserve it, but – '

'You don't!' said Karen. 'That's rubbish!'

Jessamy gave a wavering smile. 'Try telling Madam.'

Maybe I will, thought Karen; if it's not too late.

While the rest of her year were changing after Miss Eldon's early morning ballet class (Miss Eldon having pointedly ignored Jessamy) Karen slipped along the corridor to look at the notice board. The cast list for Sleeping Beauty still said:

Princess Aurora   *Jessamy Hart*

They hadn't yet crossed out Jessamy and put Ginny in her place.

Karen knew what she had to do. It wasn't going to be easy, but she owed it to Jessamy. She turned, and went slowly back along the corridor to Miss Preedy's office. Miss Preedy was the school secretary. She was the one who guarded Madam and stopped people from bothering her.

'Yes, Karen?' she said. 'What can I do for you?'

'I'd like to see Madam, please,' said Karen.

Miss Preedy looked taken aback. She was not accustomed to pupils marching in and demanding to see Madam. Madam sometimes demanded to see *them*; but that was quite a different matter.

'Won't I do instead?' said Miss Preedy.

Karen shook her head; apologetic but determined. 'I have to see Madam.'

'Madam's a very busy person, you know, Karen.'

'Yes, I know,' said Karen.

'Can you at least give me some idea of what it's about?'

'I'm sorry,' said Karen. 'It's private.'

Miss Preedy sighed. 'I'll see if I can fit you in some time at the end of the week.'

'The end of the week will be too late,' Karen said tragically. 'I have to see her *now*. It's very, very urgent.'

It was unlike Karen to exaggerate or to be melodramatic. Miss Preedy looked at her small, earnest face and came to a decision.

'Wait there,' she said. 'I'll see what I can do.'

Miss Preedy disappeared into Madam's inner sanctum. She came back almost immediately.

'Very well, Karen. Madam can spare you exactly ten minutes. In you go!'

Miss Preedy held open the door. It was only then, as she stepped through on to the thick white pile of Madam's carpet, that the full realization of what she had done suddenly hit her: she had had the impertinence to demand an interview with Madam! In that moment, Karen's legs turned to foam rubber and almost buckled beneath her. Lowly second years just didn't do that kind of thing! But she had done it, and now there was no escape. She was in Madam's room, in Madam's presence, and Miss Preedy was closing the door behind her.

'Well, Karen,' said Madam. 'Sit down and tell me what it is that is so urgent.'

'It's J-Jessamy, M-Madam.'

'What about Jessamy?'

'She's d-dreadfully unhappy and it's n-not fair because if it weren't for her I wouldn't be here and I can't j-just sit back and do n-nothing and – '

'Karen, if you have anything to say in Jessamy's

defence,' said Madam, 'kindly take a deep breath and say it as calmly and concisely as you can.'

Obediently, Karen took a breath. Trying not to gabble or stutter she told Madam the full story of how Jessamy had found out that she was trying to teach herself ballet, how Jessamy had given up her spare time to help her, how Jessamy, finally, had pretended to twist her ankle so that Karen could take her place in Coombe Hurst's end-of-term show, how Saul had come to see it and had told Belinda Tarrant, and how Belinda Tarrant had immediately arranged to audition her and in the end had offered to give her classes for nothing.

'So, you see, if it weren't for Jessamy – '

'You would not be here. Yes, Karen, I am aware of how Jessamy discovered you. I give her full credit for it. But what bearing, pray, has that on the current situation?'

Karen took another breath and set off all over again, trying, as best she could, to explain to Madam how hard it must have been for Jessamy seeing Karen promoted to be one of her specials, being given the part of a Fairy in *A Midsummer Night's Dream* while Jessamy had only been half of a peasant pas de deux, being given the lead in Snow White while Jessamy was only one of the Seven Dwarves.

'Especially,' cried Karen, 'when she's been dancing so much longer than I have and if it hadn't been for her – '

'You would not be here.' Madam permitted her lips just the faintest of faint twitches. 'What you are really saying is that she has found it difficult to cope with the idea of her pupil outstripping her.'

161

Karen blushed, deeply and painfully. When Madam put it that way, it sounded like boasting.

'I don't think I am outstripping her,' she muttered. 'Jessamy is a really good dancer. It's just –'

'Just what?' said Madam.

Karen swallowed. 'Just that I've had to fight to get here and for Jessamy it's always been expected of her, and maybe she doesn't – doesn't –'

'Appreciate it quite as much?'

Karen's cheeks flared anew. That wasn't what she had wanted to say at all!

'The question is, is it not, does Jessamy in her heart of hearts really want to be a dancer? No!' Madam held up a thin veined hand. 'No one can answer that save Jessamy herself.'

'But she was trying so hard!' pleaded Karen. 'It seems so unfair. She really deserved to have a part!'

Madam raised both eyebrows, one after another, very slowly and deliberately.

'Are you presuming to tell me how to run my own school? I think you have said quite enough, Karen. I suggest you go away now and concentrate on your own future rather than worrying yourself over other people's. Please tell Miss Preedy that I should like to see her.'

Karen tottered out on legs even more foam rubbery than when she had gone in. She had done what she could to save Jessamy, but she feared she had only made matters worse. Everyone always said that Madam would brook no interference. Now she would probably throw Jessamy out for sure, and it would be all Karen's fault.

At lunch time that day it was Karen who avoided Jessamy rather than the other way round.

'Poor Jessamy!' said Ginny, plonking her lunch down on to the table next to Karen. 'I do feel *so* sorry for her!'

'I don't see why you should,' said Lorraine. 'She oughtn't to have been going ice skating in the first place.'

'No, but I feel so dreadful about letting it out. I just didn't think!' Ginny smote her forehead with clenched fist in a seeming agony of remorse. 'I was telling Miss Eldon how I'd been taken to see *Les Patineurs* when I was a tiny child and how I couldn't decide whether I wanted to be a ballet dancer or an ice skater and –'

'Why were you telling her?' Karen said coldly.

'*Les Patineurs*,' said Ginny. 'It means, The Skaters. It's a ballet about *skating*.'

'I know that,' said Karen. 'But why were you telling her?'

'Why was I telling her? Well! I don't know. Why does one tell people things? We were just *talking*,' said Ginny. 'And then it slipped out about Jessamy, and – where is Jessamy by the way?'

Angie leaned forward. 'I heard Miss Preedy telling her that Madam wanted to see her.'

'*Again*? Oh, heavens!' Ginny threw up her hands. 'I bet she's going to take the part off her!'

'Well, that's all right,' said Lorraine, 'then you'll get it.'

Ginny turned, slowly, to look at her. 'I never thought of that,' she said.

163

For two pins, Karen could have dumped her soup bowl on top of Ginny's head.

First class after lunch was maths with Mr Underdown. Jessamy still hadn't appeared as they took their places. Karen's heart hammered and thumped. What happened if you got thrown out? Were you told to pack up your things and leave immediately? She didn't think she could bear it if she went down to the cloakroom at four o'clock and found that Jessamy's locker was empty.

Five minutes into class the door opened and Jessamy bounded through. Her face was wearing a beam that stretched from ear to ear.

'You're late!' snapped Mr Underdown.

'I'm sorry,' said Jessamy, without any signs of repentance whatsoever. 'I've been with Madam.'

'Oh! With Madam. Have you? I suppose that means I'm expected to grin and bear it. We can't say anything if you've been with *Madam*. Sit yourself down and try to look intelligent!'

Jessamy bounced across the room and took her place next to Karen. Karen pulled her rough book towards her.

'What happened?' she wrote, and pushed it across to Jessamy. By way of reply, Jessamy stuck up a thumb.

Karen snatched the book back. She scribbled, urgently, 'Are you still dancing Aurora?'

She slid the book across the desk. Jessamy looked at it and nodded, vigorously. Then she took up her pen and wrote, 'THANKS TO YOU!' and underlined it three times.

At that point, Mr Underwood walked over and took

the book away from them. He studied what they had written.

'Most interesting,' he said. 'Could we now get back to our logarithms, do you suppose?'

They did so, reluctantly. How could you concentrate on logarithms when there were still so many questions waiting to be asked?

'What did you say to her?' demanded Jessamy, as soon as they had a chance to talk.

'Oh! Just – nothing much.'

'You must have said *something*.'

'I told her how if it hadn't been for you I wouldn't be here.'

'What did she say?'

'She said ... I think you have said quite enough, Karen.' Karen imitated Madam's voice, high and querulous. 'I thought she was going to throw you out!'

'So did I! When Miss Preedy said she wanted to see me again ... honestly,' said Jessamy, 'I thought that was it.'

'What did she say to you?'

'She asked me if I really wanted to be a dancer or whether I was being pushed into it by Mum and Dad, and I said I did – because I *do* – and then she said she was giving me this one last chance and that if it hadn't been for you she would have asked for me to be removed.'

'So now we're equal!' said Karen.

'Well, not really,' said Jessamy. 'You did *loads* more for me than I did for you. I actually enjoyed giving you ballet lessons ... I bet you didn't enjoy going and talking to Madam!'

'No, I didn't.' Karen gave a little shudder at the memory.

'It was ever so brave of you,' said Jessamy.

Karen's face glowed pink. 'Oh, well!' she said. 'What are friends for?'

That evening, Jessamy rang Saul. She did it from her bedroom, so that no one could hear.

'Saul?' she said. 'It's OK! I've got the part back and I'm not being chucked out!'

'Hey! That's fantastic! Didn't I tell you? You'll always be a dancer . . . there's no escaping it. It's in the blood.'

'It didn't seem like it was in the blood yesterday,' said Jessamy.

'I guess she just wanted to give you a fright.'

'No! She meant it. It was only thanks to Karen she changed her mind.'

'Karen? I thought she was the one who shopped you?'

'Well, she wasn't! She was the one who saved me. She went and spoke to Madam.'

'Wow! That must have taken some doing.'

'It was really really brave of her,' said Jessamy.

'You can say that again! Catch me bearding Madam in her lair . . . I reckon that deserves something by way of a thank you. How about we come to watch the show, then take you both out for a meal? That'll be a thank you for Karen and a celebration for you. Do you think she'd go for that?'

'I know she would!' said Jessamy. 'Specially if she could sit next to you.'

'Oh! What it is to be popular!'

'Now, don't go and ruin things,' scolded Jessamy, 'just when you're being so nice.'

'I'm always nice!'

'Well, I suppose you are,' agreed Jessamy. '*Most* of the time.'

13

'I'm going to be sick.'

Karen announced it, white-faced and with an air of tragic finality, as she stood in the wings waiting to make her entrance as Snow White.

'Jessamy – ' She stared round, wildly. 'I'm going to be sick! I can't go on! I c- '

'Oh, yes, you can!' Jessamy pushed her way towards her through the usual clutter of bodies. 'Don't talk such *rubbish*!'

'But I can't remember any of the steps! I c- '

'You will, just as soon as you're out there, you know you will, it's happened before, it's only stage fright!'

'B-b-b- – ' Karen could hardly speak for shaking.

'Look,' said Jessamy, '*everybody* gets stage fright. Not just you. Everybody suffers from it.'

'B-b-b- '

'That's it! You're on!'

Jessamy gave her a little push. For one dreadful moment she thought that Karen really wasn't going to remember any of her steps, but of course she did; people always did. They felt the stage beneath them, the lights above them, and the old magic worked: they were away! Even if your mind went, thought Jessamy, your feet would carry on. Feet almost had a mind of their own.

It was strange, though, how people suffered from such terrible stage fright. Jessamy had never suffered from it in her life. Everybody else seemed to – but not Jessamy. She couldn't truthfully imagine what it must be like. You shook, you felt sick, you forgot your steps . . . it was all quite foreign to Jessamy. She couldn't wait to get on stage!

Mum and Dad were out there in the audience, and Saul and Ken. This was the moment that Mum and Dad had been waiting for – for Jessamy to dance a real part. Of course it wasn't a very large part, none of the student ballets lasted longer than ten minutes; but no one could deny that Princess Aurora was a leading role.

She watched as Karen stood poised for a moment *en attitude*. Wardrobe had given her a black wig, which if anything made her look even more frail and fragile than usual. There was no doubt about it, thought Jessamy, always prepared to be generous in her praise when she felt that praise was due: Karen was an extremely beautiful dancer. Her technique was secure without being in the least bit showy, her line was flowing, right through to her fingertips. No wonder people wanted to photograph and paint her. One day, when she had gained in confidence, she was going to make a truly great Giselle. For the moment, more modestly, she made a delightful Snow White. Jessamy didn't in the least mind clumping about as a dwarf to a Snow White as enchanting as Karen. After all, Jessamy's turn was to come!

Sleeping Beauty was the last ballet of the evening – 'Star billing' as a third-year somewhat jealously pointed out. Wardrobe had found Aurora a glorious royal blue tutu, a left-over from some past production of the Company, long since discarded. The ballet began with Aurora slowly emerging as from a chrysalis, the tutu suddenly springing up about her.

As there obviously couldn't be time, in ten short minutes, to tell the entire story step by step, Marguerite had been very clever and arranged the first half of the ballet as a dream sequence in which Princess Aurora remembered everything of importance that had happened to her, right up until the fateful moment when she pricked her finger and fell asleep for a hundred years.

Jessamy hadn't had as long to learn her part as all the others, but fortunately she was a quick study: every step was safely stored in the memory bank of her toes. Jessamy often found that if she tried thinking of sequences in her head, she couldn't remember them – which was a sure way to start yourself panicking, if you were the sort to panic, which thank goodness she wasn't. It was your toes you had to rely on; they would always carry you through. It was just plain silly trying to memorize steps the way you might memorize dates, say, for history. Sixteen sixty-six, Great Fire of London, 1815 Battle of something or other. Waterloo? Or was it Trafalgar? One or the other. What did it matter? Dates weren't important. Steps were. She had the most peculiar feeling in her stomach, as if a big hand were inside it, squeezing and pummelling. It was making her legs go all peculiar. All weak and wobbly. And now her knee caps were bouncing up and down. This was horrible! What was happening?

Jessamy pounded her toes in the rosin box, trying

without success to stop her teeth from chattering. This was her big moment! Mum and Dad were out there. Saul was out there. *Madam* was out there. They were relying on her. Madam had trusted her, she had given Jessamy a second chance. Oh, please, *please* –

The stage manager was waiting for Jessamy to take her position on stage so that the curtain could go up. With bouncing knees and clattering teeth, Jessamy forced herself out from the wings and crawled into the cardboard chrysalis from which she was to emerge as the Princess Aurora.

The house lights dimmed, the curtain rose. Inside her chrysalis, Jessamy began to tremble rather violently.

The music was not the easiest to follow. Marguerite had decided against the familiar ballet score by Tchaikovsky and was using something vague and wandering without any landmarks. Jessamy crouched in her chrysalis, trying desperately to keep count of the bars.

This was her bit, when it went all tinkly. The music shivered and shook, and so did Jessamy. She pulled free of the chrysalis and the royal blue tutu frothed about her.

Now came the moment. Aurora rose experimentally on to her toes, first on to the one, then on to the other, trying them out, discovering what she could do. Joy! She could stand on her toes! Exultantly, she did a little run upstage, on point – but perhaps she was being a trifle too ambitious, perhaps her ankles were not yet strong enough. At any rate, she gave a decided wobble.

Jessamy's cheeks, away from the audience, burned crimson. She caught a glimpse of Maggot and Karen, standing in the wings. Both of them had their thumbs stuck up, urging her on.

Defiantly, Jessamy threw back her head, arms upraised to greet this new world that she had entered. She flung round in a pirouette and went whirling off about the stage in a series of ecstatic leaps and turns. Self was forgotten. The miracle had occurred: her toes had taken over. She was the Princess Aurora, celebrating her birth!

'Jessamy, that was brilliant!'

'Jessamy, you were fantastic!'

'Jessamy! Oh, Jessamy!'

That last was Karen, throwing herself at her as she came off stage.

'Jessamy,' she whispered, 'I'm so glad!'

Karen was the only one, apart from Saul, who knew how much had depended on Jessamy's performance that night. Madam might give someone a second chance: she would never give them a third.

'Was it all right?' said Jessamy. 'Truly?'

'Truly!' laughed Karen.

Jessamy beamed. 'Now we can go off to supper and be happy!'

On their way out, having changed and removed make-up, they bumped into Ginny. Ginny said, 'Well, that wasn't too bad, I suppose; all things considered. A pity you didn't get a chance to learn it properly, but hopefully Madam will make allowances.'

Ginny continued triumphantly along the corridor.

'Don't take any notice of her,' begged Karen. 'She's just jealous.'

172

Jessamy sighed. 'I expect I would be, in her place.'

'Well, we can't all dance leading roles.'

'Oh!' mocked Jessamy. 'Look who's talking!'

'But it's true!'

'I know it's true. You don't have to tell *me* it's true, it's what I've said all along. Some people make it, some people don't ... you're learning,' said Jessamy, 'at last!'

Saul and Ken were waiting for them, with Jessamy's mum and dad. Karen's gran had been invited to go along but had said she 'wouldn't know what to talk about in such company', and anyway she was an old lady and needed her bed.

'I think really she's shy,' confided Karen.

'Of course, you're not!' teased Jessamy; and actually it was true, Karen was nowhere near as bashful as she had been. She chatted quite animatedly in the cab on the way to the restaurant.

'Somewhere posh tonight,' said Saul. 'No expense spared ... this is a celebration!'

'And a thank you,' whispered Jessamy, squeezing Karen's hand.

Over supper they discussed the performances. Belinda Tarrant said, 'Crits later. For now I shall simply say that I'm extremely pleased with both of you. But Jessamy, darling, I must just ask ... what went wrong right at the beginning?'

Jessamy had been hoping that no one would have noticed that anything had gone wrong, but her mum had eyes like a hawk. The least hesitation, the least uncertainty, and she was on to it.

'I thought for a moment that you were going to come off point.'

'One of my ankles suddenly gave way,' mumbled Jessamy.

Belinda Tarrant raised an eyebrow. 'Oh? That's not like you! You've never had trouble with your ankles. We'd better get that looked at. I wouldn't like to think there was a weakness there.'

Jessamy bent her head over her plate.

'I don't think you'll find there's any weakness,' said Saul. 'Is there?' He leaned across and tapped Jessamy on the back of her hand. 'Come on, own up! You had a touch of the old collywobbles, didn't you? Otherwise known as common-or-garden panic!'

'*Stage* fright?' said Karen. She turned to Jessamy, wonderingly.

'I suppose so,' muttered Jessamy.

Belinda Tarrant's face broke into a smile of triumph.

'Well!' she said. 'And about time, too! Now I begin to feel you're really getting somewhere.'

'You mean . . . you've never had stage fright *before*?' said Karen.

'No,' said Belinda Tarrant, 'she's never cared enough.'

'*Jessamy*,' said Karen. There was a note of reproach in her voice. 'You told me *everyone* had it.'

'Everyone ought,' said Saul.

'Even you?' said Jessamy.

'What do you mean, even me? I never go on stage without having a clutch at that little stone you gave me.'

'Oh, good! So it came in useful?'

174

'You'd better believe it! Everyone should have one. Their own pet rock ... and don't look now,' added Saul, 'but Madam's just come in.'

Jessamy shot a glance out of the corner of her eye. Madam was standing inside the entrance, allowing one of the waiters to take her wrap. Now she was being shown to her table, and oh, heavens! She was coming this way.

Jessamy bent her head back over her plate. She heard Madam's voice, light and gracious: 'Ben, Belinda ... Saul. Did you enjoy the show?'

It was Mum who replied for them all: 'We thought it was excellent, as always.' Mum never crawled, but even she injected a note of reverence into her voice when she spoke to Madam.

'And what of your protégées? Were they pleased with their performances?'

'Karen?' said Mum. 'Jessamy?'

For the second time that evening, Jessamy blushed scarlet. She looked helplessly at Karen across the table. What were you supposed to say?

Madam came to their rescue.

'They should be,' she said. 'I was!'

Madam tapped away across the floor on her high heels. There was a silence.

'I think that,' said Saul, 'calls for a bottle of champagne!'

BESTSELLING FICTION FROM RED FOX

☐ Blood	Alan Durant	£3.50
☐ Tina Come Home	Paul Geraghty	£3.50
☐ Del-Del	Victor Kelleher	£3.50
☐ Paul Loves Amy Loves Christo	Josephine Poole	£3.50
☐ If It Weren't for Sebastian	Jean Ure	£3.50
☐ You'll Never Guess the End	Barbara Wersba	£3.50
☐ The Pigman	Paul Zindel	£3.50

PRICES AND OTHER DETAILS ARE LIABLE TO CHANGE

ARROW BOOKS, BOOKSERVICE BY POST, PO BOX 29, DOUGLAS, ISLE OF MAN, BRITISH ISLES

NAME...

ADDRESS..

....

....

Please enclose a cheque or postal order made out to B.S.B.P. Ltd. for the amount due and allow the following for postage and packing:

U.K. CUSTOMERS: Please allow 75p per book to a maximum of £7.50

B.F.P.O. & EIRE: Please allow 75p per book to a maximum of £7.50

OVERSEAS CUSTOMERS: Please allow £1.00 per book.

While every effort is made to keep prices low it is sometimes necessary to increase cover prices at short notice. Arrow Books reserve the right to show new retail prices on covers which may differ from those previously advertised in the text or elsewhere.

Other great reads from **Red Fox**

Enjoy Jean Ure's stories of school and home life.

JO IN THE MIDDLE

The first of the popular Peter High series. When Jo starts at
her new school, she determines never again to be plain,
ordinary Jo-in-the-middle.

ISBN 0 09 997730 3   £2.99

FAT LOLLIPOP

The second in the Peter High series. When Jo is invited to
join the Laing Gang, she's thrilled – but she also feels guilty
because it means she's taking Fat Lollipop's place.

ISBN 0 09 997740 0   £2.99

A BOTTLED CHERRY ANGEL

A story of everyday school life – and the secrets that lurk
beneath the surface.

ISBN 0 09 951370 6   £1.99

FRANKIE'S DAD

Frankie can't believe it when her mum marries horrible Billie
Small and she has to go and live with him and his weedy son,
Jasper. If only her real dad would come and rescue her . . .

ISBN 0 09 959720 9   £1.99

YOU TWO

A classroom story about being best friends – and the troubles
it can bring before you find the right friend.

ISBN 0 09 938310 1   £1.95